Praise for Anita Rau Badami

TELL IT *to*

A CHAPTERS/INDI(

"Anita Rau Badami is a writer able to tra_____ _____ ___ _____ world."
The London Free Press

"The intensity of the narrative ebbs and flows and creeps."
Helen Oyeyemi, *The Wall Street Journal* (Favourite Book of 2011)

"Badami's characters are so sharply drawn they'll make a reader squirm with discomfort at the trauma they inflict upon one another. A chilling, cautionary tale at what happens when a family isolates itself against the rest of the world." *Edmonton Journal*

"The writing is beautifully descriptive and provides the reader with a definite sense of the wildness, isolation and cold surrounding the Dharma family. *Tell It to the Trees* is [a] brilliant, well-crafted novel that makes me definitely want to read more from this author."
LibrisNotes.com

"An engaging story. . . . Gripping." NoseinaBook.com

"*Tell it to the Trees* is a very creepy novel. In a brisk and economical story of a family living under the shadow of abuse, it packs more genuine spine shivers than a dozen monster horror chillers. One doesn't need to see a monster arise from a peat bog waving a Husqvarna chain saw to get spine shivers; you just need to marry the wrong man and live in the wrong place." *The Winnipeg Review*

"Badami's characters have this wonderful authenticity about them. They are neither perfectly good nor perfectly evil; they are compelling because of the balance between their weaknesses and their strengths. . . . Badami manages to combine weighty issues and historic events with the intimate daily lives of families, and bridges the distance between two countries, showing that our differences are not always as great as we believe."
Belletrista.com

"What a treat it is to read Anita Rau Badami." *National Post*

TELL IT
to the
TREES

ANITA RAU
BADAMI

Vintage Canada

VINTAGE CANADA EDITION, 2012

Copyright © 2011 Anita Rau Badami

Published in Canada by Vintage Canada, a division of
Random House of Canada Limited, Toronto, in 2012.
Originally published in hardcover in Canada by Alfred A. Knopf Canada,
a division of Random House of Canada Limited, in 2011.
Distributed by Random House of Canada Limited.

Vintage Canada with colophon is a registered trademark.

www.randomhouse.ca

Library and Archives Canada Cataloguing in Publication

Badami, Anita Rau, [date]
Tell it to the trees / Anita Rau Badami.

ISBN 978-0-676-97894-0

I. Title.

PS8553.A2845T44 2012   C813'.54   C2011-902232-X

Book design by Kelly Hill
Text and cover design by Kelly Hill

Cover images: (woman in sari) © Wendy Webb Photography;
(winter road) © Adam Radosavljevic / Dreamstime.com

Printed and bound in the United States of America

2 4 6 8 9 7 5 3 1

For Madhav, my constant

February 3, 1980

Sunday morning. Snow floats down like glitter dust from a flat winter sky, covering everything except Tree—dark against the overwhelming whiteness. The searchers have found her. Finally. She might have lain there, another anonymous mound, until spring, by which time she would have become a part of the softening earth as the snow melted in the slow warmth of the sun, if one of the search party had not noticed a pair of ravens cawing and pecking at something not too far from the house.

Part One

VARSHA AND SUMAN

Varsha

One of the searchers spotted two ravens yanking at something and walked over to investigate. I watched as he squatted and peered down at the ground, raised his arm and waved the others over. They had found her.

The birds, they told us later, were tugging at her red and gold earring that was glinting up at them. We also heard she'd taken her jacket off even though it was thirty below that night. Sounds like a crazy thing to do, but I know it's true. It's what happens before you die from hypothermia, the blood vessels near the surface of your skin suddenly dilate making you think you are on fire and so you tear off your clothes to cool down. It's quite a paradox really: the body starts to feel too hot before it dies of cold. But by that time your brain is hallucinating, creating images of longed-for warmth, making you believe all kinds of weird things. I think it would be right to assume she died happy, believing she was in the tropics, warm as toast.

She was lying not too far from our door, past the spot where in a few months, when all the snow has melted, five rose bushes with bright pink flowers and giant thorns will mark the boundary between our land and old Mrs. Cooper's. Several years ago, before she went off to live with her son in Vancouver, Mrs. Cooper sold her house to some developers who planned to turn it into a set of holiday homes, but it hasn't happened yet. It's shuttered and falling apart and I know ghosts live in it. I used to like hanging out in that whispering house, but some of the dumb boys from school discovered it and decided it was the perfect place to drink beer, smoke pot and giggle like fools and ruined it for me.

"Why on earth did she have to go out in such horrible weather?" my stepmother Suman asked for the nth time since the discovery of the body. She was stationed at the dining room window which provides almost as good a view as the one Hem and I had from the living room. "Didn't she know how dangerous cold can be? Hanh? Do you know why she did such a thing?"

She looked *stricken*. That's the word for it, the exact one. As if a giant hand had smacked the joy out of her. Not that she's a very cheerful person to begin with, but for a while this summer she'd gone back to being the way she was when she first came to Merrit's Point—young and happy. I almost feel sorry for her.

I shook my head. "We were asleep, Mama," I said gently, again. "I've no idea why she had to go out. If I was awake maybe I could have stopped her."

Beside me Hem pushed his small, warm body closer. I hugged him hard. Hemant is my half-brother, Suman's son, but entirely mine. I love him more than anything and anybody, more even than air and water and food, and just a bit more than Papa.

Out there things were winding down, the searchers loading the wrapped body onto a stretcher. We watched them carry it carefully to the waiting ambulance. An ambulance seemed kind of pointless since she was already dead, but people always hope for the best. Not me. I know that disaster lurks around every corner.

The ambulance churned away in a spray of snow and beside me Hem began to sob.

"Stop crying, you wuss," I whispered, poking his cheek with my finger. He worries me sometimes. He is too much like Suman—no backbone, all emotion and weak. I have to make sure he doesn't remain that way. For now, though, I can take it—he is only seven years old after all.

"I'm scared," Hemant said. "I wish Akka was here."

"Well she isn't, is she?" I said, even though I too miss our grandmother. She's in the hospital and not coming home. She's too old and too sick.

"What will happen now?" Hem whispered.

"Nothing. They'll take her to the morgue and a doctor will sign a certificate saying she's dead, then Papa will notify her family. That's all." For the first time it occurred to me that she also had family. Just like us. A mother and brother and two nephews and a sister-in-law and cousins and aunts and uncles and maybe a grandma like Akka.

"What if they ask us questions?" Hem's breath made a patch of mist on the windowpane.

"What if they do? We were asleep, how are we supposed to know what happened, you noodle? Now stop crying all over me, I'm here, nothing will happen to you."

He pressed closer to me, wrapped both his arms around my waist and held me tight. I love the smell of him—milky and sweet. I am not a sentimental sort of girl, but with Hem I turn into everything I do not wish to be.

"Will you always be here with me, Vashi?" He gazed up at me with his big brown eyes that unfortunately always remind me of Suman. Like a puppy begging for love, for approval, soft and silly.

"Of course, where else would I be?"

"When you're grown up also?"

"Well, I do plan to go away to university, Hem. But that isn't for five whole years."

"What if I feel like talking to someone when you're away at university?" Hem asked anxiously.

"You'll be a big boy by then—you won't need me around so much," I said.

"But I might still feel like talking to someone, then what?"

"You can always call me."

"If you aren't there?"

I knelt and wrapped my arms around him. "Talk to Tree, that'll help, won't it?" I felt his heart jumping against mine, in sync—*thump-thump-thump*—almost one. "Tree will always be here, Hem. It's ours and it will never tell on us."

I am Varsha Dharma, granddaughter of Mr. J.K. Dharma, late, and his wife Bhagirathi otherwise known as Akka. Daughter of Vikram and Harini (or Helen as my mother preferred to be called—she liked disguises). Stepdaughter to Suman, and sister to Hemant.

I am thirteen years old, almost fourteen. I love reading. I love my family. I prefer to have no friends. I plan to go to university. When I grow up I will be a lawyer. Maybe a writer. A scientist even. I can be anything I set my mind to be. I am super smart. Even Miss Frederick the English teacher who takes us for art as well and who is not fond of me concedes I am precocious beyond my years. She and the other teachers also feel I have an attitude issue—of course I do—and anger issues, according to reports they send to Papa citing complaints from the town mothers and their stupid children.

"Gene problem," Akka says. "Like your father and his father. I am telling you, Varsha, learn to control that temper. Don't turn into your Papa. Don't turn bad like him."

And I come from a long line of dead people. I know everyone in this world does, but our family tree is knotty with folk who died in odd ways, almost all of them on my grandfather's side of the family.

"We all die quietly in our own beds of old age or boredom," Akka claims. "But Mr. J.K. Dharma's people— ho, you won't believe how some of them died. I tell you, enough to fill a book!" Then she counts off her favourite deaths on her fingers. "First there was your grandfather's oldest cousin Ranjini the Raving Beauty, she who got bitten by a rabid dog before her wedding, didn't tell anyone, showed up at the marriage hall in all her finery, foaming at the mouth, had a seizure, fell into the sacred fire and terrified the groom so thoroughly that he ran out of there and never got married. And since he was an only son, his parents died without grandchildren, calling down curses on the head of Ranjini the Raving Beauty.

"Then there was that other cousin on your grandfather's side again—the one who finished a satisfying and forbidden dinner of mutton biryani at the military hotel in the Muslim area of the town in which he lived, was crossing the road to finish things off with a betel leaf stuffed with sugar beads and betel nut shavings and a touch of opium, when he stepped right into an open manhole and drowned in filth. And your grandfather Mr. J.K. Dharma, small man with a big ego, froze into a pillar of ice right outside our front door when he was forty-seven years old. He forgot his keys, came home really late, really drunk one winter night, couldn't wake me and turned into an ice sculpture. He deserved what he got, the drunken lout. He brought me nothing but tears." He was too young to die, Akka adds quickly of her frozen husband. But I can tell she's not sorry about it. He was a blot on the family name.

Last but not least is my own traitor mother Harini, who called herself Helen and hated living here with me and Papa and Akka, so she just took off without explanation one fine morning.

I don't think Papa has forgiven my mother for leaving

him even after all these years. She was a bad wife and a wicked mother, he said after she was gone. She deserved her death.

"*You* were a bad husband," Akka shouted at him. "She didn't deserve the misery you brought her and she certainly didn't deserve her death." She held me close to her and glared at Papa, who looked like he wanted to hit her the way he did my mother and sometimes me too when I am naughty.

My father controlled himself then, but he had torn up all of my mother's photographs and burned them in the fireplace. He told me I was to forget her absolutely. I was never to talk about her. Ever. She was a traitor. She had abandoned us. She was a bad wife and a wicked mother. She was an Unmentionable. We've not forgiven her, Papa and me.

But it's hard to forget. And she refused to leave me. She was everywhere in the house. I would wake up at night sometimes, sure she was sitting in a corner of my room—a loud and strong and beautiful ghost. I tried to hate her but I couldn't. I wanted to reach out and hold her tight, I wanted to rub my face against her belly, and kiss her and feel her softness. And then I'd remember that she'd left me without a backward glance, and the rage would come rushing in. I'd push her away. Not needed here, she is not. Go away monster mother, leave us alone, I'd yell, we've found somebody else to love, a new mother who will always be here, for as long as ever.

"It was your father's temper that chased your poor mother away," Akka said once. "And if he doesn't watch out, your stepmother might leave as well." She paused for a bit and then added, "Poor thing. Poor thing. She must be cursing the gods for bringing her here to this Jehannum."

I always became anxious when Akka talked like this about Suman running away. When Suman first came here, she tried so hard to fit into the space my real mother left behind, but failed every single time. That made Papa mad. And that made me worry—what if she too went away like Akka said she might. Would she take us with her? Or would she leave us behind with Papa? What if she left me and took only Hemant? After all, he is her son, I'm nothing more than her stepdaughter. Then I'd tell myself she would never do such a thing: she *loves* me. She is *mine*. Papa brought her for me all the way from India. I am grateful to her for giving me my brother and for keeping the house clean and for cooking yummy food. I try hard to make sure she has no reason to leave—I am good as gold, I help her with chores, and I hug her every morning and at night before bed. I try, I do try to make her feel loved. It is my job to tie her to me tight so that she will never ever leave.

So that's it—our family—Akka, Papa, me, Hemant, and Suman—three generations of us, crammed together, typical Indian-style, in a small house built by my grandfather on five acres of land on the edge of a rotten little town called Merrit's Point. It's in the middle of nowhere and is full of gossips and bores and kids with snotty names like Celia and Mason. If land in our town is cheap now, Akka says that when Grandfather bought it about forty-five years ago it cost less than a handful of dirt. He was dead before I was born and Akka says she has no idea why he moved all the way up here into this back of beyond. He didn't even leave a record of his thoughts—I know because I looked everywhere—just a few words scratched with purple ink in an empty little notebook: "This is all mine. Silence at last.—J.K. Dharma." What was he claiming? I asked Akka. But she couldn't tell me.

"Who knows, and why should I care?" she said. She never wanted to speak of him anyway, the frozen husband who'd robbed her of her happiness. So I have to imagine it. I imagine him living in a crowded place in India—I haven't been there yet, but I read in one of Papa's books that there are millions and millions of people there. Maybe Grandfather was tired of all those people. Maybe it didn't matter to him that he was in a place where hardly anybody else wanted to live unless they had to—like the people in town who came here to mine copper and then to work in the lumber mill. I think what mattered was that he owned this piece of the earth, paid for by him with his first savings, and when he opened a window he could hear the wind instead of a thousand chattering voices, he could see the starry sky instead of dust, and all around him his eyes landed only on quiet mountains and giant trees standing in silent clusters, bearing in their wooden hearts the secrets of all the creatures that live here.

"We are cursed," Akka wailed. "We are cursed with the family we have, and the family we have lost, we are cursed because we have to live in this town. We are cursed because we are who we are."

"If you hate it so much, why did *you* come here?" I demanded. Sometimes my grandmother confuses me with her contradictions. She loves my father, but she blames him for my mother leaving. She is fiercely protective about our family and hates "prying eyes," as she calls them, but she says my grandfather was a demon and my Papa is one too. She shoots a fist up in the direction of the sky. "It's their fault, those fancy-dress monkeys up there, those gods your silly father loves so much these days! They're blind and deaf all of them."

But even though Akka says these things about Papa and Grandfather, it is only in private, to me or to Suman. She'd never let our family down in public. Neither would I or Hem or Papa. Tight as a fist, we are, and as hard if you get in our way. Suman is the only weakness, the little finger, but Papa and I knew right away we'd have to hold her hard in our grasp. That way she wouldn't have a chance to do anything silly.

That's how we were until Anu Krishnan moved into our lives. Then everything changed.

Suman

I stood at the dining room window and stared out at the searchers in their thick winter jackets, moving around in the bleached landscape like small bright insects. I couldn't stop crying even though I hadn't known Anu that long. She'd become a good friend to me. But Vikram never liked her. I think he often wished he hadn't rented her the back-house for a whole year. And now she is dead.

Through the doorway into the living room, I could see Varsha and Hem glued to the window too. I should have stopped them from watching that horrible scene out there. Varsha glanced my way, as if aware of my gaze, and our eyes met across the space.

"Why did she have to go out in this weather?" I cried. I was repeating myself, I knew. I was not really looking for an answer from anyone.

Varsha said patiently, again, that she and Hem were asleep. "Maybe she needed to smoke, Mama," she added a second later.

I imagined Anu outside the door of the back-house, wrapped up against the cold, taking a ciggy break, as she called it. She confessed guiltily in the first week following her arrival that she smoked like a chimney. "I know, I know," she'd said, catching my disapproving look. "I will probably die early from lung cancer."

"No, no, I wasn't thinking of that," I replied quickly. "Just that Vikram doesn't like anyone smoking inside the house. So . . ."

"Aha! So you don't care if I burn up my lungs and die, eh?"

I had smiled uncertainly. It was years since somebody had teased me, laughed with me instead of at me.

Anu had held up a hand. "I give you my word of honour, I shall never smoke inside the house. You can assure your husband of that." She kept her promise, even when the weather turned cold and the leaves began to fall, and then the snow. I should have warned her that the cold could not be trusted, that it was a dangerous thing.

My name is Suman Dharma. For thirty years, from the moment of my birth until I left for Merrit's Point, I lived in one of four streets that form a quadrangle around a famous and very old temple in Triplicane in the city of Madras. People believe our neighbourhood has been around since the first century BC. Since then, it has seen crowds of foreigners from Portugal, Italy, France and England, but has somehow managed to retain its past. It still has the feeling of a small town frozen in time, even though it has become, in reality, just a tiny corner of a large, bustling, modern city. Our home was on the third floor of a rickety old building and in order to get to it you had to enter through the living room of the ground-floor tenant Rama Shastri, a priest at the temple, slapping aside damp bedsheets and pyjamas, striped underwear, dhotis, saris, petticoats and diapers, dozens of them, that always hung like banners from the low roof, as if to celebrate the teeming life within that small space.

Our own home was kept scrupulously clean by my father's sister Madhu Kaki, who was a tyrant with the broom and the mop. Even so, she could do nothing about the tired outer walls of our building which needed to be whitewashed, or the windows with streamers of old paint hanging away from their slowly rotting wooden frames, their iron bars pockmarked with rust. She would set me to scrub the paint away with a rough ball of wire, and leaning out of the window to reach a curl of paint I would gaze down at the many strands of gullies and streets and roads, messy as hair on an uncombed head, life of all kinds swarming like lice on them. From the lowest fly to the almighty human, no one creature was more superior than the other from the high vantage point of the windows in our building. Or, for that matter, from the perspective of thieves and goondas, politicians and religious nuts, who killed both flies and humans with the same casual brutality. We were all packed into those filthy streets, animals, insects, rogues, saints, demons, breathing the gummy air, and neither minded the other. We humans had learned to walk those streets like gods, omniscient, with eyes and ears all over our heads, always aware of that steaming pile of cow or dog shit to be avoided, the rickshaw or the scooter, the car or the bullock-cart, the thieves and the beggars, the touts and the vendors. We saw and heard everything and negotiated our lives through it all without too much damage to our bodies or our souls. I can say with complete certainty that despite the dirt and the chaos and the lack of any finery, we had that one thing that most people spend a lifetime looking for and never finding: happiness. I was a happy girl and it is perhaps that deep and sturdy foundation of happiness that has sustained me this far.

Occasionally, small groups of tourists, lost in the maze of narrow streets and whirling crowds, wandered into our street and I would wonder what they saw when they looked at us and our homes. After I came to the West, I understood that air of panic and wonder that surrounded those tourists—the world they had left behind was a planet apart from the one in which I grew up. They would twirl around, their heads dizzy from an excess of everything, the pulsating, vibrating, chanting, shrieking chaos, from the confusion of stories constantly forming and dissolving before their dazzled, dust-rimmed eyes. They would go *click-click-click* with their beautiful cameras, ask passersby to lean against this wall or that as they clicked, searching always for that authentic moment, the absolute truth, the unimaginable multicoloured reality which they could never catch no matter how hard they tried. They failed to understand that the truth was a shifting, shy thing, like sunlight changing from moment to moment, unknowable even if you spent your life in the heart of it. The secret, as my beloved father used to say, was to watch for it from the corner of your eyes, pretending that you weren't really looking. That way, you might, if you were lucky, catch a glimpse of truth.

Once, near the temple tank, a group of tourists asked if they could take a picture of me and my aunt Madhu Kaki, and so my photograph went out of India before I did, into the wide and foreign world. Somewhere out there in Germany or England, Italy or America, I live in the pages of a stranger's album of family photos—a girl of sixteen with hope in her eyes and the trustful certainty that nothing could go wrong.

Varsha

I can remember back to when I was four. Okay, not much, just bits and pieces. It was a sunny morning. Spring was in the air. I could smell it. Papa had taken Akka to the hospital in Vancouver and I was in the car with my Mom. I had no idea where we were going. For a pizza, I hoped, or hot chocolate or a movie—anything was possible with Mom. But we kept driving till we were right out of Merrit's Point in another town. I don't remember the name. We went up a narrow street and stopped in front of a small house. Its front garden was piled with snow and nobody had shovelled the driveway. Mom was tense with excitement. I could actually feel it.

She said, "Stay in the car, I'll be back in a second. Don't get out, did you hear? I'll be mad if you do. I won't bring you with me again, ever."

I asked her, "Who are you meeting?"

"A friend. I have something important to discuss with him."

"Why can't I come in with you?"

"You can't. We're talking big-people stuff." She checked her face in the rear-view mirror, patted her hair.

That made me feel cross and I started whining. "I'm thirsty, I want some water, I want to come inside too. I'm cold."

Which I guess made her cross. "Here's some water. Now stay here and stop being such a baby," she said. She thrust a bottle of water at me, slammed the door shut. She opened the door again and kissed me. "I'll be back soon, promise."

I watched her ring the doorbell, and got a brief glimpse of a man with red hair at the open door. Then Mom disappeared inside and I was all alone.

She was gone for hours. She said it wasn't hours, only twenty minutes, but it was. I bet it was. I waited and waited for her to come out of the stranger's house. I was really bored and then I was really angry. I wondered if I dared to leave the car and run away. Or maybe I'd just get out and scream for Mom and everyone would hear because the street was very quiet. That would show her! I imagined telling Papa about it, but she'd made me promise and I knew I never would. So I waited. And waited. Then I started getting scared. It was almost noon, I think, and we were far away from home and pretty soon Papa would be back with Akka and find us gone and get real mad at Mom. Maybe at me too for going with her. Or simply because I looked like her. Or something.

I'm not sure why Papa always gets so angry with me. Back then, it wasn't my fault that my Mom sometimes took me with her when she got an attack of the roamings. Roamings, that's what she called them. I would watch her carefully, but they'd come sneaking into the house, wrap themselves around her feet and carry her off to the shops or to the next town, and even farther sometimes. She'd always get home just before Papa did so he wouldn't know.

When Mom felt the roamings getting closer, she'd pick up the phone and call Mrs. Cooper next door and ask her if she minded coming over to keep an eye on me and Akka. But if she couldn't then Mom called Aunty Chanchal for help. She *didn't* like to do that because Aunty Chanchal is a snoopy old bag and wanted to know where Mom was going and when she'd be back and why and what and who and other stuff that Mom got cross about. There was also the danger that Aunty Chanchal would spill the beans to Papa. Her husband Uncle Gopal is Papa's friend and Aunty Chanchal considers Papa part of her family.

Mrs. Cooper, on the other hand, only wanted company and couldn't be bothered less about what Mom did. All she cared about was a hot cup of tea and a nice long chat with Akka. They used to be really good friends until her daughter got pregnant and ran off with somebody and after that Papa didn't encourage her to visit much and always got mad when he discovered Mom had got her to help. So Akka and I stopped telling him when Mom had the roamings and Mrs. Cooper came over. That way, Akka said, there was no room for a quarrel, or for Papa to holler and Mom to holler back and threaten to go away for good from *this godforsaken hellhole of a place.*

Every six months, Papa took Akka to the hospital in Vancouver for a complete checkup. They left very early and got back in the afternoon. Mom called this her "independence day." She'd be full of a suppressed excitement the night before and in the morning took forever to dress. She'd wait for Mrs. C. to show up, give me a kiss, promise me a treat if I was a good girl who knew to keep secrets, and then disappear for the whole day.

But that morning, Mrs. Cooper couldn't come to babysit and my mother had to take me along with her on her roaming. I sat on her bed and watched her transform herself from a Mom into a Princess. She emerged from the bathroom in a pale satin slip the colour of her skin, with a towel wrapped around her head. Dimly visible through the thin satin was the dark V of her crotch. She unrolled transparent nylon stockings, holding out her arms to draw them up her legs, and when she bent down to pull them on, her breasts swelled out of her brassiere like living things. I remember the faraway expression in her eyes as she delicately stroked the hose up her smooth brown legs, up and up and up, first one then the other. At last she straightened up. Her hands went under her slip to make some quick, secret adjustments, and she was done. She caught me watching and raised an eyebrow at me like the Hollywood divas in her magazines. She laughed. She had a lovely laugh, as nice as the tinkly wind chimes Akka had hung on the lilac tree in the front garden.

"What are you peeking at, you naughty girl?"

I giggled and she looked away. I know now she was already detaching herself a little more each day, preparing to leave me, although I didn't realize that then.

She gazed thoughtfully at her image in the mirror, stroked her fingers through her damp hair and dried it carefully around a big cylindrical brush until large loose curls bounced about her head. She trapped it down under a hair band and applied foundation to smooth out an already smooth skin. Then she picked up her powder compact, a beautiful silver thing with some fancy stones set into a design of roses, which appeared mysteriously one day and which she said she would give to me on my sixteenth birthday. There was a condition, though—I was not to tell Papa about its existence.

"It's a secret, between you and me," she had said, kissing the top of my head as I played with the compact.

"Where did you buy it from?" I asked, and she winked at me conspiratorially.

"I didn't buy it," she said.

"You stole it? You found it finderskeepers losers-weepers?" Mom had an amazing talent for finding things lying around—beautiful things, expensive-looking stuff—the compact, a bracelet, a purse made of silk and beads—so many pretty things, all secrets from Papa, all promised to me when I turned thirteen, fourteen, fifteen, sixteen.

"I don't steal things, silly," Mom said. "I *find* them." But I was not to breathe a word about her amazing luck either to Papa or to Akka. This was our secret—between us girls. I was not good at keeping secrets, I needed to tell someone, but when I went to Akka, she stuck an index finger in each of her ears, squeezed her eyes shut and said, "No, no, I don't want to know anything. I am too full of my own secrets, I will burst if you give me any more to keep!"

Akka didn't want to be like the woman in a story she told me once, a kind woman who listened to everybody's secrets and kept them safe inside her belly. That way people would feel light as air and good as gold because they didn't have their secrets weighing on their souls. But the poor woman grew fatter and fatter and fatter from all the secrets inside her and one day she exploded like a great big balloon with too much air. All the secrets were released and flew around the world. And everybody knew everything and so the people to whom the secrets belonged got mad at the kind woman and cursed her so hard her spirit got no peace and is still wandering around the world trying to collect the scattered secrets.

"But Papa will get mad if I tell him. What should I do?" I was frantic. It was like holding on to an urgent pee.

"Go tell the trees," Akka said. "They won't tell a soul."

Sometimes Mom said she'd bought these things *cheap* at the second-hand store in the next town, or if it looked too expensive, like with a pair of old and intricate earrings, she said she'd inherited it from her great-grandmother. I knew she was lying.

Mom liked people to think she was grander than she really was, that she came from an old and respected family, the kind that lived in big homes with polished wooden

floors and crystal vases full of chubby pink roses. She
dropped hints about ancestral property, heirlooms, an
inheritance. But I never once met my grandparents or any
cousins, aunts or uncles on my mother's side. It was as if
she had sprung out of the earth rootless, with no past, no
memory, no history except what she made up. She turned
up her nose at Papa, called him a great big bore, she joked
about his work as an accountant in a small lumber mill
which he always says is very important work. Her sneer-
ing drove him mad, he'd lift up his large hands, shout and
throws things like a crazy man.

"At least I earn an honest living," he'd roar. "You just
live off me, you bitch."

Papa likes an immaculate home. My mother was a
messy bessy—she hated being a housewife, she grumbled
when Papa complained about the piles of clothes that
grew like they were alive in all the corners of our house:
heaps of frilly panties on the dining table waiting to be
put away, shirts needing to be ironed lurking about on
top of the washing machine, dirty clothes stuffed into
baskets, socks, underwear, her beautiful frocks . . . they
came tumbling out from all over. Mom was always sniffing at them to check if they were clean or dirty, cursing
under her breath if they needed to be washed. Nothing
was ever in the right place—hair clips on the couch and on
the coffee table, high-heeled shoes on the stairs and on the
landing, bras, books, barrettes, lip gloss, socks, my clothes,
Papa's underwear, magazines, everything was everywhere
and always in the wrong place. She was a wretched cook

and even though she followed recipes faithfully, some-thing *always* went wrong and the end results, though available in vast quantities, tasted horrible. She'd start boiling something, forget it on the stove because she was busy reading a book or getting dressed to go out, and end up with a burnt pot of food. It drove Papa crazy, but she never changed her ways.

They'd scream at each other, getting angrier and angrier, until I was sure the house would shatter.

"Why did they get married if they hate each other?" I'd ask Akka when I was a little older. In all the fairy stories she told me, the prince and the princess fell in love, got married and lived happily ever after.

"No, no, your Papa loved your Mom more than any-thing in the world," Akka would say. She was his religion, my grandmother explained. And he was like a wild-eyed and fanatical believer. It was his love for her that ate away at him, turned him into a maniac. And the more he loved her, the more he wanted to hold on to her, the more she wanted to get away. And that made him screaming mad. It was terrifying. I was glad I had Akka to go to when our house turned into a volcano.

So that morning when I was four, I waited in the car for my mother and wondered what she was doing inside the house. Two girls walked past, a car came up and stopped at the house across the street and a man and a woman got out. They held hands and went inside their house. I wished they were my parents. I wished my Mom would hurry up.

Then just when I started to cry the door opened and there she was. She was shining like an angel, I thought. She got into the car and leaned forward to kiss me. "Here, this is for you." She held out a small bag with some candy.

I crossed my arms and refused to take the bag. I was angry with her, but also glad that she was back. That she hadn't left me forever inside the car in a strange town.

"Oh come on, come on, who's my sweetie pie? Hanh? Hanh?" She tickled me and I giggled. I loved her again.

Around her throat was a pretty new necklace.

"Can I have that too?" I touched her warm brown skin.

"When you are sixteen, baby." She smiled. "But only if you don't tell anyone about it. Especially Papa."

She smiled again and kissed my cheek. My anger floated away. Mom drove super fast down the roads, the wind tearing through the windows which she liked to keep open, turning my hair into a big nest of tangles. I felt we were on a roller-coaster ride.

But it was no good. By the time we got home, Papa was already there. He was madder than a hornet. "Where were you two?" he shouted as soon as we stepped into the house.

"Out," Mom smiled at me. "We went for a picnic, didn't we, baby?"

I nodded. I didn't look at my father in case he caught the lie hiding in my eyes. I felt bad for him. I understood exactly what he must feel like when he looked at Mom, this lovely restless butterfly who never entirely belonged to us. I think I knew, even then, that she would leave us as soon as she could convince herself that it was all right to go without me, her only child.

"Where was this picnic? What did you eat?" Papa grabbed her by the arm and shook her. "Why do you lie to me? You are lying, aren't you? Aren't you?"

"You're a tyrant," she yelled. "I'm going to leave you one of these days, I promise!"

"I'll come after you and kill you," he shouted back. He would rather she died than leave him. At least that way nobody would look at us with knowing pity, he said, at least we wouldn't have to live with the shame of her, and the shame of being abandoned.

Shame is a big deal in our family, we all have an obligation to the Family Name. This, in my imagination, is a great invisible god, multi-armed and many-headed like the ones Akka describes in her stories, who looms over all of us with thunderbolts at his fingertips and a river of poison waiting to be unleashed from his great black cave of a mouth.

"Don't be silly, Vikram," my Mom said, shaking him off as if he was an annoying insect. "It doesn't suit you."

Papa slapped her then, hard, across her face. She rubbed her cheek, her eyes filling with tears. She stared at him and said in a quiet voice, "I told you never to do that again. I hate you."

Akka limped out of her room and gathered me in her arms. "Stop it, both of you," she begged. "Please, for the child's sake. Stop."

"Ask your son to stop," Mom said. "He hits me. And you do nothing. You should be ashamed of yourself." She stormed out of the room and up the stairs and into my bedroom. The door slammed and there was silence.

Akka pulled me into her room and shut the door. She was crying silently. I was glad she was there. I crawled into her bed and she wrapped her arms around me. "In the morning it will be okay," she whispered. I could feel her warm tears on my face.

The next morning Mom didn't come out of my room until after Papa had left for work. I heard her moving around upstairs for a while and when she came down, she was bathed and dressed and carrying a small bag. Her face was swollen, her eyes bright.

"I'm stepping out for a bit," she said. She leaned down and kissed me on my forehead. "Be good."

"Is Mrs. Cooper coming to look after Akka and me?" I asked. I noticed she had no lipstick on. It made me anxious. She never went out without lipstick. She hadn't washed her hair and made it fluffy and pretty either—it was bunched up in a ponytail.

Mom hesitated, and then said, "Yes, she will be here in about half an hour. You look after your grandmother till then. Can you do that? Are you Mom's big girl?"

I nodded. Akka just looked at Mom but didn't say a word. I wonder if she knew Mom would never return.

When Papa got home that evening he found a note from her on the dressing table in their room: "I can't stay. I am sorry." It was written on a piece of paper decorated with a border of purple and pink flowers. I had made six of those decorated notepapers for her birthday. For weeks I held on to the idea that she had used it deliber- ately—a secret message to me to say she would come back for me. I like to think that. I like to think that if she had not died taking a corner too fast, if that truck had not been speeding down from the opposite side, if and if and if, my mother would have returned for me.

Later that night there was a knock on the door. It was the police. When they'd left, Papa said, "Better she is dead than shamefully alive. Better for us." Then he began to weep, big gulping sobs, like a baby. I had never seen my father cry.

But the next day he said, "Enough, I want her out of here." He got some garbage bags and filled them with Mom's things, even the earrings she had promised to give me, the jewelled compact, the silver rings I liked so much, the necklace she'd got from the strange man's house the day before she ran away from us. He spent a whole day ripping her out of all our photographs. And when I said I would like to keep the ones of her and me when I was a baby, when she loved me, he smacked me hard.

He started to pray every morning and in the evening too. Akka says it's to help him hold on to himself. I imagine my father without his gods, falling apart, arms and legs and head and feet breaking free and whirling around our house, hitting everything in a fury. I'm glad the silver gods in the small room next to Akka's can keep him tied together.

Three months after Mom's death, Papa's gods ordered him to find a new mother for me and so he did. He went to find a wife in India, somebody like Akka, who will never leave him. It was the first time Papa had gone to India.

"He's a fool if he thinks anybody will stay with him in this hellish place," Akka muttered.

Aunty Chanchal moved in with us to help because Akka was too old to look after me on her own. Papa stayed in India for a month and returned home full of secret triumph. Six months after that, Suman arrived.

"A present for you," Papa said, pulling her into the house, a short woman with long curly hair and worried brown eyes.

That night, before going to sleep, I asked him, "What if she too goes away like Mom did?"

My father gave me a serious look. "It's your job to make sure she doesn't, Varsha. And that's the last time we mention Helen, do you understand? From now on, Suman is your Mom."

I call her Mama. My Mom is too close, too real still for me to transfer the name I used for her to a stranger from India. Suman doesn't mind. She is just anxious to be my mother. She is glad, I think, she doesn't have to fight with me for a space in our house like those fairy-tale step-mothers. She works hard to love me, she combs my hair like a proper mother even though I am perfectly capable of doing it myself now at thirteen, she fixes me breakfast and makes sandwiches for my lunch box, she folds my clothes and neatens my room. This has been very nice,

especially since I don't remember Mom ever doing anything like it and I love it. Then she gave birth to Hemant,
a son for Papa, and I thought we would be happy as the
sun in summer.

But.

Papa can't forget. Mom was beautiful, Suman is not.
Mom yelled back at my father. Suman wasn't quiet at first,
but now she doesn't talk very much. Papa began to find
fault with everything she did or didn't do. He shouted at
her, he called her a fool, and he told her she can't wear
anything other than saris. Akka said he is ridiculous,
forcing the poor woman to wear saris in winter. Papa told
Akka to keep her nose out of his business. She told him
that if he didn't watch out, he'd lose another wife. That
Suman is a good woman and he should consider himself
lucky to have her. Papa told Akka to shut up.

Suman's stopped smiling and cries a lot. She doesn't
sing when she does the housework the way she used to.
She's stopped telling me funny stories that her father told
her when she was a little girl. She's become silent as the
walls and talks only in whispers when she has to, which
makes Papa even madder and she cries some more. She
still cooks all morning and cleans the rest of the time.
She dusts, wipes, mops every single day, sometimes twice
a day. I never see her without dusters and rags, brooms
and buckets. You can eat off the floor of our house,
perform surgery on it. The hum of the vacuum cleaner is
our daily music. Papa will never love her. She does everything Papa expects her to, but he refuses to show when

he's pleased. He never comments on the things she's done, always looks for the things she hasn't. He makes surprise checks sometimes—he runs a finger across the tops of bookshelves, behind the spice jars in the kitchen cupboards, on top of picture frames, places that most people might forget to clean. If he finds a bit of dust, he swipes it up with a finger and holds it out without comment and Suman shrivels up like a slug. And then she gathers herself together and she starts all over again. She cooks up a feast of his favourite things, irons all his shirts, cleans the house until it sparkles like a jewel, dresses in her best clothes. Nothing works.

She's become a bit mean. I think she's maybe stopped loving me. Now she complains to Papa about me. Maybe she hopes Papa will be mad at me and forget about her. So she goes whisper, whisper, whisper. She's like a brown mouse scurrying around carrying tales. *She refuses to eat her breakfast, it is not good for her to go to school hungry like that, I don't know what to do with her, I try so hard, she lost her gloves again, what to do, she is so careless this child, I am finding it difficult to manage.* Sometimes it works. Papa's eyes fall on me instead. Nothing makes him feel more godlike than to discover our wrongness. Nothing makes him more heartbroken than to beat my naughtiness out of me, and more happy than to forgive me afterwards. He is doing it for my good, after all, he has no desire to see me turn into my mother.

"VARSHA, COME HERE!"

"VARSHA, WHERE ARE YOU?"

"WHERE IS THAT WRETCHED GIRL?"

Then the belt whistles through the air to scorch my back or legs, hidden places nobody can see. Never my face, he is careful about that, Papa, always concerned about other people's opinion, always worried about our family name. What would people think if they saw belt marks across my face? It would never do, not at all. The Dharmas are spotless, ab-SO-lutely perfect.

Afterwards Suman always feels so bad. She cries and kisses me, combs my hair. She says, "I am sorry, I am sorry. How could I tell him? I don't know why I told him. Oh poor child." And I hold on to her hard, glad she is there, that she still likes me after all, grateful for the soft-ness of her touch as she examines my bruises and soothes them with a towel wrung out in ice water. "It's okay, Mama," I say, stroking her face. "I deserved it, I was a naughty girl. It's okay."

Akka is on my stepmother's side. She can't bear to see her unhappy. I hear her telling Suman that she should leave. "Run, girl, run as far as you can," she says.

Once she offered Suman her gold necklace to go away. I adore my Akka, but I was mad at her for doing that. "Why did you tell her to go?" I asked. "She is mine."

"I can't see her suffer, pearl of my eye," Akka said. "It is not right."

I was real scared afterwards. I didn't want to lose my new mother too. So one day I took her passport from her dressing table drawer. I taped it behind the photograph of my dead grandfather. Suman will never dream of looking there. You can't go anywhere without ID. She doesn't have a driver's licence, so the passport is her passport out of this place and now she doesn't have it. I catch her sometimes, looking, looking, *looking* for that passport, and when Papa asks her, irritated as all heck by her fidgety looking, what on earth she is searching for, Suman shakes her head and mumbles that she is not. Not searching, only tidying up. After a while she gives up, and I breathe a sigh of relief. She isn't going anywhere. I am glad. I will try to love her as if she is my real mother, I promise Papa's gods and Jesus Christ and Gandhi and Martin Luther King and all the good guys up there who might be listening. Suman *is* my real mother. I will love her to death and make sure she never ever leaves us. Never. Ever.

Suman

Until my marriage, I had travelled out of Madras only occasionally: with Madhu Kaki to Tirupati a few times so that she could pray for the welfare of our family to her favourite deity, and once when I was seventeen on a school trip to see the Taj Mahal. The only reason I was allowed to go was because I would be staying with my friend Lalli at her grandparents' home in Agra.

Lalli's father was a merchant whose family had descended to Madras from northern India years ago and had settled there. He owned several small corner shops that sold magazines and sundry items like biscuits, batteries, cigarettes. Although Lalli spoke my language fluently and could easily pass for a South Indian girl with her long oiled braids, her flashing dark eyes, her clothes, her accent and gestures, the inside of her home was a foreign place for me. There were several families living together in that large home with its barred windows and narrow corridors opening into numerous small bedrooms— Lalli's parents and her three brothers, two uncles and their wives and children, and several other indigent relatives who cooked and cleaned and worked for the family in return for a roof over their heads. The women were soft-spoken, unlike my own noisy Madhu Kaki, and drifted around with their sari pallus draped over their heads, shadowing their faces so that I could never figure out who was who except by their whispering voices, like wind rustling through leaves. Their continuous state of quiet busyness became frantic in the evening when the men returned home and had to be pampered with tea and juice and snacks and inquiries after their day or their health.

Most of the time the women wore simple starched cotton saris, but once a year they would all explode into a passion of colour, dress up like brides, even the oldest of them all, an aunt who was in her sixties, to celebrate a festival called Karva Chauth when prayers were sent up to the god Shiva for the welfare of their husbands. I had heard about this festival from my friend, who always brought us trays of sweets made for the occasion, but had never really seen anyone performing it until my trip to Agra where Lalli's grandparents lived in a quarter of a crusty old building in one of the many dark gullies that criss-cross that city like veins in an ancient body. On the second night of our stay, all the women in the building began to prepare for Karva Chauth.

"Come on, let's go and join them," Lalli whispered mischievously, pulling me up the narrow stairs to the terrace on top of the building.

"Are we allowed to?" I whispered back. "Isn't this for married women only?"

"Yes, but who is going to know?" Lalli had pulled her sari pallu over her head. She grinned at me. "Come on, what are you scared of?" She pressed a small round mirror into my palm. "Don't look up at the moon when it appears, look at it in the mirror."

"What will happen if I look at the sky instead?" I asked, mystified by this exotic ritual. We had our own rituals, but familiarity had made them ordinary.

"You will have a hundred years of bad luck," Lalli said dramatically, and giggled again. "If you believe such nonsense!"

It was the first hour of the night and all around, on the terraces and balconies of Hindu homes which grew like mushrooms out of the dank filth of gullies, were other women waiting, like Lalli and me, to glimpse the sharp crescent of the new moon as it fell from the sky into their mirrors. It was forbidden for them to stare up at that silver C of light—I have no idea who forbade them, or why. No doubt some ancient seer, one of those bad-tempered, long-bearded old fogeys whose potent curses turned their wives into stone, their daughters into heaps of ashes or trees or birds for small transgressions— no doubt it was they who decided that a woman was not to look straight at the silly moon. It would be a wicked thing to do. No, worse, it would bring harm down on the hapless heads of their husbands, those idle gods who sat inside their homes, stuffing their bellies with food, and yelling out orders while their poor wives fasted for their well-being after slaving over the kitchen stove to turn out meals fit for maharajas.

And so we stood there, with mirrors in our hands, to witness the birth of the new moon. Not too far away, despite the darkness, I could see the dome of the Taj Mahal thrusting up at the sky like a pale breast. I gazed at my face dimly reflected in the mirror. *I.* Such a sliver of a word to hold the meaning and the matter of all that I was and would be. I believed that I was tougher than that frail stick of a word, I could leap over its scrawny boundaries, I could become more than I was.

Not too long after our trip to Agra, Lalli was packed off with a dowry of five lakh rupees and two dozen gold bangles and a Godrej refrigerator and a motorbike for her husband, only to end up hanging from the rafters of her new home, the mehendi from her wedding still wet on her palms. Her in-laws wailed and beat their breasts and said that a mentally ill girl had been passed on to them without their knowledge, but the rumours that swept around the gullies were that her mother-in-law wanted more gold bangles and her father-in-law wanted an air conditioner, and her new husband wanted a car instead of a scooter. When Lalli's father refused to oblige, her in-laws strung her up like a criminal hung for murder. She had murdered their desires.

I wept hard for my lost friend, swore that such sorrow would never come to me. Before Lalli's wedding, I had sat at her mehendi, a swirling vineyard of dark green henna paste drying on my hands, turning red from the heat in my blood (the hotter your blood, the redder the colour left behind), and wished that my father too had the money and the jewels to bribe a man to marry me. I was eighteen—a ripe old age for a woman, practically a toothless crone, if the talk around me was to be believed. Until Lalli's death I had convinced myself that marriage was the best thing that could ever happen to me. Not surprising, really, given that marriage, marriage, marriage was all those wretched gully-people thought about when they saw a girl. Not just in my gully, it seemed to me, but in every road and alley, every single home throughout the country. The economy of India runs on marriages. Weddings are big business. All you hear right through the year—except for a few months when Saturn presides over the planets and nothing auspicious is launched—is talk of marriages. Every activity has to do with that walk around the sacred fire. Saris are purchased, jewels ordered, and money flows around like so many intersecting rivers. Fortunes are built (by shopkeepers and marriage halls, priests and cooks) and lost (by the girl's parents, mostly) during the wedding season. Gold prices all over the world are affected by this season—going up when we are getting married and our poor parents are spending their life savings on gold ornaments, and collapsing in the bad-luck months of July, September and December.

And in those fallow months when nobody is getting married, mothers and aunties and grannies and matchmakers exchange horoscopes and plot yet more weddings for the coming year. Even the songs that Madhu Kaki sang to lull me to sleep when I was an infant were about how a prince would come and carry me away from my father's home if I was a good girl and shut my eyes tight. When I was naughty and refused to eat something, my aunt would threaten me with spinsterhood—that curse more dreadful than death even. She would warn me that nobody on earth, not even a crow, would wish to make me his bride if I carried on fussing. And when I was older, women on our street would pull my nose and say, ayyo, this is growing too long, who will marry her? Raddled old grandmas who had nothing to do but dream of love and young bodies mating, and of men with tight muscles, would squeeze my small breasts and cackle, soon, soon, it will be time for a man to touch these, for a baby to pull at these. Or they would pinch my cheek and yank my chin and warn me that if I went out in the sun like an ignorant cat, my skin would grow too dark for matrimony.

By the time I was twenty and out of college, I had developed a ringing in my ears and a buzzing in my head from all this talk. It drove me mad.

I still wanted other things then—to study some more, to find a job like those women who sprawled confidently inside the glossy covers of magazines in Lalli's father's shop, to travel to strange places with names like New York, Trafalgar Square, Down Under, the Arctic and the Antarctic. I wanted and wanted and wanted everything that was out of reach. I was like a donkey, chasing a carrot dangled before its greedy nose, like Tantalus, that man in a Greek story that our English teacher Miss Shanti told us. This man was punished by the gods, who, it seemed, were like the angry sages in our myths who forbade women to look directly at the new moon.

On that night of the new moon, though, I, along with all those women who stood around us on the terrace in distant Agra muttering prayers for the health of their husbands to Shiva the Lord of the dark and of all the ghastly hordes who roared through the mysterious place between waking and sleep, between night and dawn, real and unreal—I too sent up a prayer to the wild-haired, ash-clothed God to send me a husband who would carry me away from my small life in one of the back alleys of the world. Shiva the eternal bachelor had been pierced awake from cosmic slumber by an arrow from the God of Love and had fallen fiercely in love with Parvati. I too imagined myself a Parvati, or a Mumtaz Mahal, a Juliet or a Laila, the object of a hero's undying love. I too wished to be borne away on horseback, in a train, or a plane, even in an ox-drawn cart if nothing else was available, by a man who would allow me to expand beyond my boundaries, beyond that stick-insect of an *I,* who would show me the world, who would love me into being more than what I was. It did not occur to me that I needed no one to take me to my ambitions, to fulfill my desires. I could do it on my own, like Chandra did, and the women in those magazines in Lalli's father's shop. All I needed was the will and a little bit of courage.

My excuse was the world in which I was raised. Even though my own childhood and youth was far less constrained than Lalli's, I was part of a tight-knit, contained universe where everybody lived within an unwritten code of conduct the knowledge of which came to us with our mother's milk, was dinned into our skulls at every opportunity by our elders, inhaled from the virtuous, dusty air we breathed. In this world secrets could never be kept. Homes were set so close that young boys jumped from one rooftop to the next without fear of falling in between. You could look into your neighbours' windows, stretch a leg and an arm and climb in. When windows were shut, everyone knew it was because on the other side a couple was making love or they were quarrelling or somebody was dying and wanted a little bit of quiet darkness in which to slip away from the world they had inhabited for this while.

If it wasn't the closeness of one house to another that kept us all within the unwritten code of conduct that nobody dared to break, then there was the fear of alienation from the community. Forgiveness was not part of our vocabulary and to be cast out of our close-knit community was akin to being disowned by your own mother, or, in my case, my father—an unbearable thing. It was like being exiled from the world, sent out alone into the unknowing silence of outer space. It filled me with fear.

There were, of course, the occasional transgressors, bold creatures like Chandra Raman who went around with a swing of her round hips and her nose in the air seemingly unaware of her disgrace, or if she knew, careless of the whispers following her. Somebody had seen her on the beach with her cousin Shekhar, holding his hand no less, so close to him that you could not even pass a blade of grass between them. That was enough to destroy her reputation, although Shekhar, the cousin, had got away scot-free. Chandra became a pariah on our street, and even though she continued to live there, she might have been a ghost the way people looked right through her.

I was a girl of thirteen when Chandra was cast out, and even at that age, when my prudish moral compass was set by my elders and the people in my neighbourhood, even then I had smarted at the unfairness of it all. She had been like an older sister to me, had taken care of me innumerable times when my mother was ill and Madhu Kaki, who had moved in by then, was busy with housework. Chandra had held my small, shivering body when my mother had finally died, insisted on walking me to school every day for nearly a year until I got somewhat accustomed to the idea of death's permanence, to the notion that my mother was not coming back, that I would never again hear her weak little voice calling me to her except in my memory or in dreams.

But to my everlasting shame, I had done nothing. I did not even wave back when Chandra fluttered her hand at me as she went past our house, her bangles shining in the morning sun, their jingle abnormally loud in the dusty, watchful silence of the street. Instead I ducked inside and hid there until Chandra had turned into a bright blur of sari at the other end of the street.

This is my weakness, I know that now. I am a follower of rules. I do not have the courage to break them. I cannot bring myself to fight back against the things I know are wrong or to stand up for things that are right. I let Chandra go. I watch as Vikram beats the children and I do nothing. I am that scrawny little stick-insect of an *I* that fell into a mirror on a crescent-moon night many years ago on a terrace in Agra. I am still there, unable to climb out.

I moved away from the window and glanced at the children again. They were huddled together, whispering. Hem appeared to be crying.

I walked across to them and they shrank closer to each other. "Come away from that window, both of you," I said.

They nodded and moved away. Varsha had her usual pleasant expression, polite but guarded. I have no reason to complain about her behaviour—she has always been the perfect child, young girl now, no longer the five-year-old I met when I first set foot in this house.

"You shouldn't be watching such things," I said. "I should have stopped you. Hem, come here, bayboo." I held out my arms. Hem hesitated, glanced at his sister. I caught the edge of something odd in the look that he received from Varsha. What was it they were hiding? Some childish secret, perhaps? I have to catch Hem alone—he will never tell me anything when his sister is around.

Varsha looked back at me with her fathomless black eyes and said quietly, "Hem is scared of dead people. He hasn't seen any, that's why. But I told him it's okay, I'm here for him."

Where does the girl get her self-assurance from? It's not as if she has seen dozens of dead bodies herself! I held out my arms and insisted, "Come here, Hem."

He didn't come to me. He shrank against his sister. "I was asleep," he whispered.

What was he talking about? I felt like pulling him away from Varsha and holding him against me. But before I could do anything, as if she had read my thoughts—and perhaps she had, the odd girl that she is—she pushed Hem towards me. "Go to Mama, Hem. She will make you feel better. And I could do with a hug as well, Mama. I am scared too. To think poor Anu was right here, so near our house . . ." And her eyes brimmed with tears.

I was surprised by the sudden display of vulnerability from a girl who hardly ever weeps, not even when Vikram whips her. Then they were wrapped around me, both of them, the girl as tall as I am, her freshly shampooed hair soft and sweet-smelling, and I was ashamed of my suspicions. She is still a child at thirteen, she has done everything since I came to this house to make me feel a part of her family.

"Mama," she whispered, her breath tickling my ear. "Our Mama, we've nothing to be scared of as long as you're here, right, Mama?"

I nodded silently and thought of a morning a few years ago when she was eight years old. Hemant was a toddler. Vikram had left for work after scolding me for something I had done or not done, I don't recall. I couldn't stop crying that day although I did make an attempt to control myself when I was in Akka's room, making up her bed, folding her clothes.

"Why do you stay, Suman?" the old lady had asked me unexpectedly. She was in her chair, her legs stretched out on a stool, and I was massaging some warm oil into her wrinkled old feet. "Go, leave today. Run. Run."

I stared up at her and the tears started up again. "How? I have no money, how can I leave? Where do I go?" I asked. "And my son, I can't leave him."

Akka leaned forward and touched my cheek and said, "Take your jewellery to a pawnbroker, sell it. And here, this is to get you to a city with pawnbrokers." She dug around beneath the seat of her chair and fished out a handful of dollar bills which she thrust at me.

I looked down at the money—not more than a hundred dollars. And my meagre collection of jewellery would get me no more than two hundred. That was barely enough for a flight back to India, definitely not enough for me and my son to survive on. Akka had no idea how much anything cost, Vikram took care of all her financial needs like he did mine, doling out money to

me when I wanted something, insisting on a full account-
ing afterwards, driving me to town to do our weekly
shop together.

"Well, what is the matter? What's going on in that
head of yours?" Akka asked.

"This is not enough for anything, I can't leave," I said.

She fumbled around her neck, removed a gold chain
that she always wore and pressed it into my hand. "Then
take this too, I don't need it."

Still not enough, I thought. I stood there mutely, terrified of leaving, terrified of what might happen if I stayed.
And Akka pushed me with all the strength left in her with-
ered arms and said, "Are you a sheep, are you a brainless
ninny, what are you doing standing there like that? Go,
I say, go!"

"Mama is going away?" Varsha had entered the
room unnoticed and stood there, a tiny girl with large,
frightened eyes. "Akka, you are sending Mama away?
Why? I don't want her to leave. She is mine. She is mine.
She is *mine*."

The girl hurled herself at me and wrapped her
arms around my legs. "I won't let you go!" she screamed.
"I won't. I'll tell Papa! I will, I will!"

It took an hour to convince her that I was not leaving
and after that Akka never again brought up the subject, at
least not when the girl was around.

A few days after that, my passport vanished. I assumed
Varsha had told Vikram about my conversation with
Akka and he had taken away my passport to prevent me

from leaving. I didn't dare to ask him for it. Who knew how he would react?

Was Varsha aware of my renewed plan to leave? With Hem and without her? I would like to take her with me, but I can't, she's not mine to take anyway and she wouldn't leave her father. He comes first in her affections along with Hem and Akka. Had she sensed it somehow, like an animal smells unheard, unseen things?

Now, with Anu gone, I wondered if I would have the courage to go after all. I held the two children close. My ear filled with the sound of Varsha's quiet breathing and I felt guilty that I do not entirely like her.

She pulled away from me and stared into my eyes. "I love you, Mama," she said. "Please don't leave me."

I was silent. She shook me and insisted, "Don't leave me. Promise you won't?"

"I promise," I said, the lie tripping easily off my tongue. "I promise."

Varsha

I was already in a bad mood thanks to Nick Hutch, who'd gone on and on about me and Hem being POCs.

"What's that?" Hem asked.

"A Person of Colour," Nick said.

"As if you aren't, Nick Hutch," I retorted from my usual spot in the bus, the rear window seat right at the back, far away from all the dumb kids from our school. Nobody ever takes that seat, or the one for Hem beside it, even when I'm late getting out of class. Everybody who has any sense knows it's my seat. Everybody remembers how I nearly killed Warthog a couple of years ago, even though he's three times my size and could have pulverized me. Warthog had called me a dirty name so I stuck his face in the snow and sat on his head until his legs stopped kicking and he nearly suffocated. Of course I got in trouble with the principal who called Papa to school and told him that I had anger management issues and would be expelled if I attacked anybody else. Warthog's mother was there too, all teary and accusing. I cried and told them what Warthog had called me and added that he'd tried to molest Hem, which was why I reacted the way I did. It was a whopping big lie but it worked. Nobody was very fond of Warthog—he doesn't wash and he smells bad, so it was not difficult to convince Mr. Russell that he was a pervert.

I stared Nick down. "You're a POC too," I said. "You're pink as your Mom's bum, Nick Hutch, so watch what you say about others." But I wasn't really in the mood to pick on Nick. He says dumb things but he isn't a bad guy.

"Oh look, what's that thing there?" Nick turned away and pretended to be engrossed in something outside the window. He can't bear it when I make fun of him. He would like me to be his girlfriend, but I am not his girlfriend and will never be. He wiped his hand across the foggy window, jammed shut forever, cloudy with old dust and layers of child-breath, jammy hands and spit, and pointed to a small heap of flowers glowing like red coals against the new green of the field we were passing. There was a cross too, sticking up like a raised hand.

"*Look*," Nick insisted. I peered out of the window, my hair blowing into my eyes. The bus created a wind and stirred up dead leaves that flew like butterflies. Then the sad little cross was invisible, and the road behind was just a long stretch of emptiness, not even another car on it, not even a bird.

"Somebody just got killed there," Nick said. "And

that's a cross to show where the person died. That way god can come get his soul."

"Could be *her* soul," I pointed out.

"Could be," agreed Nick.

I know he has a crush on me because a few months ago he offered to pay Hem four dollars and thirty-two cents, all the money he had in the world, to steal a pair of my hair clips, my socks, anything. My brother reported this to me, of course. He can't hide anything from me.

"Tell him he would have to pay you twenty-five bucks," I instructed Hem.

"Won't Papa get mad at us for selling your stuff?"

"How would he know? Are you planning to carry tales to him? Hmmm?" I gave Hem my special LOOK which really scares him. Then I relented. "Think of the things we could buy with twenty-five dollars. You could get that book and kit on how to make your own snow, if you wanted to."

But there was no way Nick could get so much money. Joe Hutch is always watching him. He caught him one Christmas pinching a dollar from his pants pocket. "My dad socked me for stealing, but I wasn't really, it was to buy him his Christmas present," he'd complained, nursing his sore ear.

I just had to laugh. "You stole money from your dad to get him a present? You are a moron, Nick Hutch!"

He gave me a pained look. "I was just borrowing it. And he would have got his rotten dollar back along with three of mine anyway—that's how much his present was going to cost. But he didn't even want to hear me."

I'd laughed again. Nick can be an idiot, but he's also funny and the only one who gives me birthday presents, even if they are kind of weird and useless. At least he remembers.

I hung halfway out of the bus window, and looked back, searching for those red flowers in the distance. I felt sad. We have no crosses or markers for our dead—we burn them. If we didn't, there would be one for our grandfather, Mr. J.K. Dharma, and one for Vasant, Suman's baby who died because he was born prematurely. Suman had named him for Spring, her favourite season, even though he was only the size of a tadpole when he died. Sometimes when I close my eyes, I think I can see him. I tell Hem this and he starts to cry. He is such a wuss. It is so easy to scare him. "Really? Really truly? You can see ghosts?" he asks. And I say, yes, yes I can. I can see my dead Mom and Grandpa and our baby brother. I tell him if he doesn't listen to me and obey me and love me always, I will call the ghosts to take him away to the other side of our gate where they all live. Or to the bottom of the lake. Now when we pass the lake on our way to the bus-stop, Hem always walks on the far side of the road. But I only scare him sometimes, when I want him to obey me and he doesn't.

I think it would be nice to have a marker or something where I could place bunches of fire-red flowers—for my dead brother anyway. Instead of a cross, perhaps

I could stick a statue of Papa's favourite god Ganesha in the ground. How strange would that look, a dancing elephant-man in the middle of nowhere c/o Merrit's Point? That's what I would like when I die—a god stuck in the snow to look after me for all eternity.

"My baby brother died too," Hemant said as if he had jumped into my head and stolen my thoughts. "But we didn't put up any crosses."

"That's because we cremated him, Hem," I said from my corner of the bus.

"I don't know anyone who's dead. What did your brother look like?" asked Nick.

"Like a dead baby. What d'you think?" But I didn't actually see my dead brother, only pictures of fetuses about his age in a medical book I looked up in the library. He was ten weeks old, so he had dots for eyes and small hands and feet. I felt like crying when I saw the pictures, but I didn't. Papa would have been ashamed of my weak nature. The baby died on my twelfth birthday, which came and went unnoticed because Suman fell and the baby started coming and the ambulance had to be called. And while we were waiting Suman kept telling us, "I fell down the stairs, silly me. I tripped over my slipper. If anyone asks, don't forget, I fell down the stairs."

Then Papa held her carefully like she was a piece of precious glass. He asked her if she was comfortable and she smiled at him even though her eyes were full of tears and nodded yes, I am fine, yes, I am fine. But I knew it really hurt.

Aunty Chanchal came to look after Akka and Papa drove me and Hem to school before going to the hospital. At the school gates Papa got out to open the back door of the car. He hugged both of us and said, "Be good, children, I love you."

Hem didn't say anything back, but I did. "Love you too, Papa." Even though I knew. He got back in the car, looked out of the window at us and waved. We waved back, our hands high in the air. It's what he likes. It's what he expects. A fond farewell when he leaves and a fond greeting when he returns.

After the car had disappeared down the road, I smacked Hem's head. "Why didn't you say anything? He'll be upset. Just hope he didn't notice."

"I hate Papa. He hurt Mama," he said.

"He didn't hurt her. She hurt herself, didn't you hear? She tripped over her slippers and fell down the stairs."

"No she didn't," he said. "He pushed her out of their room. We saw it."

"No we didn't." I smacked his head again.

"Yes, we did," Hem insisted.

"Okay. But he didn't push her. She tripped on her slipper and fell on her own. And you are not to mention it to anyone. I'll call the ghosts to punish you if you do."

"What if it comes out of me by itself?"

"Hold on to it, it's a secret. Hold on and tell it to Tree when we get back from school, okay?"

"Why does he beat Mama? Why does he beat us? Doesn't he like us?"

"Of course he does, silly. He loves us, wants only what is good for us. That's why he has to punish us when we're naughty. For our own good."

"Was Mama naughty?"

"Papa didn't do anything to her," I reminded my brother. "She *fell*, Hem. Fell. On her *own*." He was a baby. He needed to be taught how to keep secrets. Family secrets. *Our* family, *our* secrets. Nobody else had to know.

We reached our stop and the bus ground to a halt in a cloud of dust. The doors folded open and Hemant and I got out. Mr. Wilcox the driver waved and took off down the road, farther and farther, until the low roar of the bus became one with that of the wind which always blows down from the mountains through Merrit's Point.

There was no sign of Suman. Later she apologized humbly, but we were mad at her, Hem and I. It's her *job* to come and get us. That's what mothers are supposed to do—look after their kids, make sure they're safe. Anything could happen to us between the bus and the house, *any*thing. That's what Papa says, although Akka thinks it's ridiculous. She says I'm old enough to bring my brother home myself and that Papa is being a tyrant for making Suman do it when she has so many other things to attend to.

"Where's Mama?" Hem asked, looking around as if she might be hiding in the fields on either side of the road.

"How should I know? Come on, let's go," I said. "Maybe Akka is ill or something."

Hem squatted down on the ground. "I'm going to wait. She's always here. She said she would always be here no matter what!"

"Come on, Hem, don't be a giant squib!" But I was worried too. It was so unlike Suman not to be waiting for us—she's there every day, sun or snow. What if she had had one of her fits of illness? What if she'd fallen and broken her arm again? Or if Akka had finally died, as she kept hoping? I started to walk homewards fast, dragging Hem behind me.

"Do you think she's dead?" He sounded tearful.

"I don't know," I snapped. "Come on, hurry up and stop behaving like a baby."

We passed old Mrs. Cooper's house, the only other home on that long road. It's shuttered and silent now. I always wish, when we pass the house, that Mrs. Cooper's granddaughter, Gilly, was still around. She's the only friend I've had. After moving to Calgary to live with her dad, she sent me a single letter. Then I heard nothing more from her. Mrs. Cooper moved away a few years ago as well, to live with one of her sons—Billy or Dave. They were both construction workers and Mrs. Cooper told us stories of how they spent the winters in the ski resorts nearby, busy renovating, maintaining or building the posh hotels and cottages that had grown up around the resorts. They came home every weekend to be with her, sometimes bringing beautiful girls with long legs who walked with a swing and a sway of their tiny hips. Once I tried to copy the walk to entertain Hem, swinging awkwardly around the house, one arm bent at the elbow and hand glued to my waist, my nose in the air, until Papa noticed and slapped me about the head for being silly. Good thing he didn't figure out who I was mimicking—I'd have been beaten black and blue for sure. Papa used to remark that the girls looked cheap, like tramps, even though they had seemed perfectly nice to Hem and me. Even Suman had liked them, but then she likes everyone. Papa says that she has no *discernment*. Afterwards, as always, he was sorry for smacking me. But as he explained over ice cream treats the next day, it was only to teach me the difference between good and bad, dross and gold. Poor Papa, it's not his fault that he has to be hard with me sometimes. I know he's worried I'll turn out like my real mother, the one who abandoned us to our fate.

So I always stare at the shuttered windows of the Cooper house when we walk past. They're like dead eyes. When Mrs. Cooper was there, even after Gilly had left, she'd watch for us to go by, sometimes call us in for some fresh-baked cookies, and we would run up her driveway guiltily. And Suman would follow, saying, *Only one cookie each, hurry up, and don't tell Papa, don't tell.*

In winter, the old lady would keep the living room lights on warm and friendly as her smile, and reassuring, informing us that we were only about twenty minutes from home, not lost in the wilderness of snow that spread out in every direction, borders and edges blurred and lost.

"It's a long time now. I don't think she's coming back, do you?" Hem said, thinking my exact same thoughts again, like he's my twin.

"Don't know. I miss her."

"Me too. Her cookies were the best in the world."

"Greedy little thing, all you can think about is food." I yanked his arm. "Race you home. Last one there is a miserable, bandy-legged spider."

I swung my bag over my shoulder and started running. We slowed down out of breath as we approached the gate. Noticed the car parked outside.

"I wonder who that is," I said. The car looked crappy, worse than ours, which Papa calls his *rusty steed*. Sometimes my father can be really nice and really funny.

Hem started running again and barged through the front door. "Mama! Mama! Where are you?"

Sounds of laughter floated out of Akka's room. I thought, would they be laughing if someone's hurt? We dropped our bags and went into our grandmother's room. There was Suman, sitting on the bed, cool as you please, and Akka, leaning against the pillows piled up in her chair, her white hair like silk threads spread out on the pale pink covers. And a tall woman we'd never seen before.

"Hello, hello, you must be the famous Hemant! And this lovely girl must be Varsha," she said. She held out her hand. "I am Anu Krishnan."

I didn't know how to react to that. Nobody has ever called me lovely. I wasn't sure what to say or do, so I frowned at the woman to let her know I wasn't about to be taken in by praise. Later on, when I read her notebook, I knew she was a smiling liar.

But I have to admit, she looked kind of cute, and her clothes were really, really nice. Her hand was still out, but I decided not to shake it, just because. Later on, after I read those pages from her notebook, I was glad that I didn't take her hand. She was no friend. She was a liar, Anu Krishnan. She never meant a word of anything she said to us. How was it she described me in her horrid book? Ugly little thing, teeth like her grandmother's coconut scraper, beady eyes. And Hem was a troll, pretending to be sick all the time. And Suman needed help to get away from us all, and she, Anu Krishnan, outsider, was going to give it to her. Oh yes, she lied and cheated and planned to steal.

In the meanwhile, my dear little brother was doing his bit to make Suman feel miserable. He threw a hissy fit and believe me, nobody does that better than him.

"Why weren't you there?" he shouted, near tears, glaring at Suman, ignoring the stranger. "I thought you were dead."

"Don't be silly, Hemu." Suman looked embarrassed. Akka was startled. Anu Krishnan was smiling as if my brother was a comedy show. "Why would I be dead?"

"THEN WHY WEREN'T YOU THERE?" Hem hollered. Once my brother gets going, he can be spectacular.

"I said I was sorry, Hemu." Suman walked over to him and knelt beside him, looking worried, the way she usually looks.

"Stop shouting, Hemant," Akka said sternly. "What is there to be scared of? Your sister was with you."

"Mama said there are strangers on the roads, she said they do bad things to kids. She said she'd always wait for us. I WAS SCARED!"

"I said I am sorry! It will never happen again, I promise." Suman reached out again to hold Hemant, but he pushed her away and stalked out of the room with me in tow.

Behind us, Suman said, "I am so sorry, I don't know what has got into my son. He is normally a good little boy, isn't he, Akka?"

"Yes, he is," Akka agreed. "But I think he is getting a bit spoiled by you, Suman. They can walk home by themselves, at least in summer. Varsha is thirteen, old enough to take care of them both. And why have you filled their heads with nonsense about bad people and kidnappers and rubbish like that? There is nobody around for miles here."

We waited, crouched on the landing at the head of the stairs, Hem and I. Heard chairs scraping backwards in Akka's room. The woman's voice. "I think I've held you all up for long enough. If you give me the keys, and point me in the right direction, perhaps I could find my own way?"

So that's who she was—our tenant for the back-house, which Papa had decided to rent out.

Suman's voice floated up: "I'll walk you there. Show you where all the things are . . ."

Then Akka's. "And when are you coming back to see me, Anu?"

I was startled. Akka sounded *friendly*. What was wrong with her? She is usually so sensible. Suman, yes, you can count on her to be daft about everybody, but our grandmother said she always took her time to get to know people.

The tenant laughed. "Whenever you want me to, Akka. Your wish is my command!"

Suman looked up and spotted us hovering on the landing. "Varsha, Hemu, do you want to come with me to show Anu the back-house?"

I held Hem's wrist hard. We were not going anywhere. We were not going to speak to Suman. She had to be punished for neglecting us, her children, in order to spend time with a stranger. I stared down at Anu, standing behind Suman, tall and threatening, as if she already owned *my* stepmother and *my* house, and *my* Akka. The woman stared back.

"We shall hate her forever," I whispered to Hem.

"For ever and ever," Hem repeated solemnly.

Suman

I came to Merrit's Point nine years ago at the end of March, a time when the ground is knee-deep in snow, and your breath hangs like a ghost before your face. I had flown from Madras to Vancouver. From there a single-engined plane that shook and rattled as it thrust through enormous cloud banks brought me to Merrit's Point, once plunging into an air pocket with such sickening violence that I was sure that we were about to crash. I was one of five passengers on the shuddering twin-engine plane, and the only woman. The four men who sat scrunched up in their seats, knees wedged against the seat in front, their large heads nearly touching the roof of the plane, were like giants. What did they eat to make them so big? Vikram, my husband, was tall, but his head was long and slender, not like these men with their football-shaped skulls. I wondered what they thought of me—a bright exclamation mark in my yellow and black printed silk sari. I was also wearing all my jewellery because people back home, those with relatives abroad, had warned me that it was better to carry my valuables on my person because suitcases were often stolen by luggage handlers. From their talk it seemed as if the world beyond our dusty street was full of thieves, smugglers, rapists, hoodlums and other criminals.

Mountains circled the quiet little airport at Merrit's Point, looming over it. There were only a few passengers waiting for luggage. I dragged my two suitcases off the carousel and loaded them on a cart. Both had blue plastic rope wrapped thrice around them, giving them the happy look of birthday presents. It was Madhu Kaki's idea. My aunt was certain that bags travelling on planes to foreign countries regularly came apart at the seams.

"Remember my sister-in-law's nephew's son Gopi, who arrived in the U.S.A. and received his belongings in bits and pieces?" she had said a week before my departure. She was bent over one of her six steel trunks that her father had given her as part of her wedding dowry, searching for a rope of the right thickness and colour. There was nothing that she couldn't fish out of one of those trunks of hers: measuring tapes, geometry sets that had belonged to her sons, packets of seeds whose names she had forgotten and that she had collected from the garden of her late father-in-law's house, stacks of saris which she was saving to sell to the raddhi-wallah, waiting for the gold prices to peak before she did so, because the saris, she claimed, had pure gold borders and she was determined to get the best price possible for them. There were tins of powder that had belonged to her long-dead mother and that she could not bear to throw away, photo-graphs, ancient flowers from her bridal braid, six pairs of scissors, silver bowls and plates, ripped-up cotton saris and bedsheets, and dozens of other odds and ends for which she always managed to find a use.

She poked me on the head with her knuckles. "Well, do you remember the boy?"

"I can't say I do," I had replied, preoccupied with the thought that I had got married in too much of a hurry. I had wished that Chandra Raman was around to tell me how to deal with my fears, how to toss my head as defi-antly as she had tossed hers and run away from my new Canadian husband.

Madhu Kaki rapped me again with her knuckles. "He was the one who would have come first in the All India Medical entrance exams, that brilliant he was, but forgot to write his student number on his exam paper in his hurry to hand it in and poor fellow had to enrol in a polytechnic instead. Ended up as a chef in a hotel chain, the top chef, I am told. Now do you remember who I am referring to?"

The nephew had eventually gone abroad, but since he had no aunt like mine to find him bright blue rope to tie his suitcases, they had exploded en route, leaving a trail of clothes and other belongings at various airports. Finally, only six of ten pairs of VIP P-front navy blue underpants, which the young man's mother had packed into the case, six (out of sixteen) vests (with sleeves because the young man sweated a lot and the arms of his shirts suffered as a result), one of several tins of mango-lime-ginger pickles especially made for him by his grandmother, and a single shoe had arrived at the end of his journey from the east to the west of the world. His other shoe, a winter jacket bought at great expense from a smuggler who operated out of a radio repair shop on Second Beach Road, and numerous books which he might have needed were all lost when the bulging suitcase gave way.

Madhu Kaki narrated these details with such certainty that I believed her. Besides, she and other members of our extended network of friends and relatives in Triplicane told and retold the story of the boy's baggage so many times that even if it was not entirely accurate, the endless reiteration gave it the shine of truth.

I had known Vikram for less than a month before our marriage and wasn't sure whether it had all been a dream—the good-looking man who had been brought home by my Appa one fine morning and who had asked for my hand in marriage in a week. Such romance was unheard of in our mundane lives, such passion was the stuff of cinemas. Now I know that neither romance nor passion had played a role in Vikram's decision. He chose me because I am good-natured, easygoing, the perfect substitute for a wild dead wife, a patient nursemaid for his aged mother, a caring mother for his child. He gauged me correctly. I am the staying type, the sort who can be made to fit a mould, the sort who will always do what is expected of her. But I did not realize, until I came here, how afraid and docile I could become, how easy to push around.

Our neighbourhood could not stop talking about our marriage for the entire six months that I remained in Madras after my wedding. The gossips and the match-makers, whose noses had been put out of joint by this alliance which they had not arranged, went around telling everybody how cunning my father was. "Pretends not to know anything about anything," they whispered about my unworldly Appa, who had never harboured a single devious thought in his entire life. "Who would have believed? He must have planned it all in advance. Caught a fine cockerel for his little chickadee! And a foreign-returned one at that!"

Vikram was a distant relative of our front-door neighbour Ganesh Maamu. He was visiting India for the first time in his life and had somehow missed the party of relatives that had gone to the airport to receive him. Appa—on his usual Saturday morning rounds of the temple, the vegetable vendor, his friends at the Dramatic Society of Triplicane, the lending library—had found Vikram wandering around the crowded market near the temple, sticking out like a palm tree in a mango grove, stopping occasionally to check a map of Madras that he held. Vikram's taxi hadn't managed to locate Ganesh Maamu's house and had dropped him off at the temple instead.

In his khaki trousers and T-shirt, he had that gloss of Abroad on him, down to his clean, baby-pink sandal-clad feet that looked like they had been hidden from the sun for years, and his way of looking you straight in the eye

which some of the elders in our area mistook for a lack
of respect. Appa knew who he was, of course. Everyone
in our locality, on all the four streets forming a square
around the temple, had been made aware of his visit,
his exact and convoluted relationship to Ganesh Maamu,
why he had never visited India before (these things
happen what-to-do), what his father had done for a living
(something to do with wood but dead for many years),
what Vikram did (something brilliant, no doubt).

Faces lined windows at the hour when the Foreign
Boy, as he had come to be known, was to be borne
home from the airport by Ganesh Maamu and his relatives, mothers busy in their kitchens had posted their
young children at their front doors and shouted every
now and again, "Have they come?" and the street urchins
were all on alert to spread the word as soon as they
descended from the two cars that Ganesh Maamu had
borrowed from somewhere. The arrival of a long-lost
relative, and an eligible man at that, was a matter of great
ceremony, and so everybody in Ganesh Maamu's house
had gone to the airport.

Besides, it was an opportunity to gawk at the planes
as they took off and landed. We were all avid plane-
spotters on our street. We all yearned to go away somewhere far from home, yet few had dared to leave the
familiar sanctuary of our streets. So plane watching was a
substitute for travel. We were fascinated by those winged
creatures that roared overhead late at night and early in
the morning. "Plane! Plane! Come and see, quickly!" the

lucky spotter would yell, and everyone would rush out onto their verandas and balconies hoping to catch sight of that magical creation that could take you across the world. And sometimes, soon after the monsoons when the weather was cool, families got together and went on picnics to a spot near the airport. Mothers and aunts and older sisters would unpack tins and paper packets full of puris and curd-rice and lemon-rice, and we would all lie on our backs or lean back on our elbows, tilt our heads backwards until we developed cricks in our necks, and watch the mid-morning planes taking off, vapour trails streaming out across the light blue sky like the tails of exotic birds. These were the small pleasures of our lives. So the arrival of the nephew many times removed, who was coming from halfway across the world in one of those silver machines, was a moment that belonged to us all courtesy of his family here on our street.

It was surely Fate, evil thing, that led my Appa to Vikram as he stood there poring over his map, trying to figure out which of the maze of lanes he should plunge into. And Fate that had brought the man to our home. I wish now that Fate had left us all alone.

I don't remember what I was doing when he arrived, carefully stepping around the rangoli that the cleaning woman had drawn in the dust outside, stooping to avoid the fresh mango-leaf torana decorating the door lintel. He had stood there blinking as his eyes adjusted from the sharp sunshine outside to the cool darkness of our front room.

I remember that he kept those eyes on me right through the visit, following my movements as I served lemon juice and freshly made chakkuli, his face intense and serious. I was aware of his gaze even after Ganesh Maamu and his fifteen family members came rushing in to retrieve him, somewhat put out that we had claimed him first.

In the days that followed, Vikram came frequently to our house. On one of those occasions he smiled, a rare occurrence, and told me that I looked like a blossom in my pale orange cotton sari. Nobody had ever likened me to a blossom even though that is what my name means. Madhu Kaki never failed to remind me that I was nothing like the beauty my mother was. (My aunt was fond of attributing rare talents and amazing beauty to the dead.) I don't blame her, she was merely doing her job, which was to keep me a modest young woman with no great ideas about myself or my appearance and no correspondingly high expectations of anything so that I would never be disappointed by what life or the future had to throw at me. One of the match-makers had remarked that I was not bad to look at but she didn't know how to describe me. There was nothing she could praise to high heavens—not my colour, or my eyes, or any other aspect of me. I could neither sing nor dance and I was a middling student with a degree in Home Economics. Nor did my father belong to a famous or wealthy family which might have whitewashed all my deficiencies and added the necessary gloss required for an advantageous marriage. By the time Vikram came along

I was nearly thirty, at peace with my ordinariness, and quite resigned to remaining at home with my aging father and aunt. I made a small income from coaching schoolchildren in math, reading and writing, but my needs were small and it was enough. I was happy.

When Vikram flattered me, compared me to a flower, I should have been wary because there was nothing floral about me. If I resembled anything botanical at all, it would be a banana leaf—plain, sturdy, useful. But I was as unaccustomed to male flattery as a person who has never touched alcohol. How easily I lost my head. Now, with bitter hindsight, I believe that when he looked at me he saw a woman who could be moulded, who would not rise up and complain, who would be submissive to his needs and the needs of his household, who would not fight back, as Helen had done.

Within a week of his arrival he asked Appa for my hand in marriage. Ganesh Maamu's wife came bearing the auspicious platter of fruit, the betel leaf and the coconut. She was smiling even though everyone knew that she was put out by Vikram's insistence that he wanted to marry me—she had talked a lot before he arrived about an alliance between him and her daughter. Ganesh Maamu too had tried to throw a spanner in the works by informing my father that Vikram's first wife had left him before she died and that he had a young daughter from that marriage. There was also an invalid mother who needed to be looked after. My father was doubtful about the match when he heard about the child.

"I don't want you to spend the rest of your life taking care of me and your aunt, although I would be happy to see your beloved young face every day until I die," he said, stroking my head the way he used to do when I was a little girl in need of comfort or advice. "But I am not sure I want you to travel thousands of miles with a stranger to look after his child and mother. The decision is yours, but don't do anything at the cost of your happiness, Sumana."

Then Ganesh Maamu came up with the notion that it would not do for Vikram to get married without his mother's consent. But when my father contacted Akka, all she had to say during their short telephone conversation was, "It is up to the young woman, whether she wants to marry my son or not. I have nothing to say except that I will welcome anyone he brings home with warmth. That is all I can offer—a warm welcome."

"Must be a very *modern* type of woman," Madhu Kaki commented when this information reached us— approximately five and a quarter minutes after it had hit the Triplicane air—in a tone that implied that she must also, therefore, be crazy. How could any mother allow her son the freedom to choose his own wife? Marriage was a serious business, involving a lifelong commitment on the part of two families rather than of just two individuals. It was well known that mothers could see what their sons could not. Sons were prone to blindness when it came to women, even ordinary ones such as me.

"But then, she was always a strange girl. I remember her from when we were young together," Madhu Kaki said, musing about Vikram's mother who had grown up on this same street a long time ago. "Beautiful creature, no wonder her son looks like a film star. Insisted on going to college. Unheard of for a girl in those days. Her parents were freedom fighters. They had strange ideas about bringing up their daughter. There were young men from the best families lining up to marry her, but guess who she selected—a fellow from an unknown family. I don't even know where they met—in college perhaps. She married him and a few years later we heard they'd gone away to Canada. Not a word from her since, all these years. And now suddenly her son is here about to become your husband. How strange is life!"

On my wedding day, my father gave me a few small pieces of jewellery that had belonged to my mother. "This is your mother's blessing, your insurance against bad times, my beloved child," he said, pressing the soft velvet pouches into my hands. "Which I hope you will never have to use."

On that beautiful autumn morning, when the notes of the nadaswaram swelled out joyously over the wedding guests, when the mridangam players slapped their hands hard against the leather stretched tight over their drums in a rising crescendo to signal the auspicious moment when Vikram tied the thaali around my neck, I would never have believed that I might one day contemplate selling my inheritance to strangers in pawnshops halfway across the world.

Varsha

Another memory. Stronger this time. I was almost seven years old. It was a cold, clouded morning in December. Snow floated down like flowers from a low grey sky. Papa was at work, Akka was dozing in her room. And I can see me: I am on the floor of the book-room working on some drawings. This room is special. It's too small to call it anything as grand as a library, but it's where our father reads to us some evenings after dinner, his voice, which I think of as being a sort of golden brown colour, and warm as toasted marshmallows on a cold evening, comforting as milk and cookies, carrying us into the worlds hiding inside those books. Our family photographs live on the walls: my grandfather with a black mouse of a moustache perched over his chubby lips, standing straight as an electric pole behind Akka who is seated and is resplendent in wedding finery, her beringed hands holding down her knees as if she's afraid they might kick up and down and run away with her; Papa, grinning and missing two teeth, about Hem's age in one picture, solemn in another with a graduate's robes and a degree roll in his hand, ready to go out into the world and light it up with his brilliance; Suman, wearing giant dark glasses that hide most of her face, her mouth painted pink and fixed in a tight smile, with Papa a handsome prince, arm draped around her shoulders like a python, his fingers, a bunch of bananas, hanging over her right breast; and finally one of all four of us, smiling as if our lives depended on it. Behind this you can see the space where my real mother's photograph used to hang before Papa ripped it off the wall and threw it away. Sometimes when the new picture of Papa, Suman, me and Akka goes slightly crooked, I know it's my jealous Mom fidgeting behind it, wishing she'd never left.

This is the room where the Punishments happen, where Papa's belt cuts through the air and lands on my calves, or where I wait with bated breath while he checks my report card. Is he going to smile, or will he frown? Pat on the head or punishment? A sweet or a slap?

That morning Suman was perched on a stepladder in our book-room, dusting the books, her enormous stomach pressed outwards, her hair a mess of curls around her face. She's expecting a baby, but I know she's not happy about it. I heard her crying in Akka's room the day she found out.

A cow mooed somewhere above me. A cow? Inside our house? Am I imagining things? Is it my real mom being a clown, trying to get my attention? She was always one for attention, my mother, always wanting people to look at her, to admire her, to tell her how beautiful she was. But she wouldn't moo, it isn't elegant. I looked up at Suman. She was gazing absently at the opposite wall and seemed not to have heard a thing.

"Mmooaw!" she said suddenly. "MMOWAAW!"

She was holding on to the bookshelf with one hand and touching her belly with the other. An expression of alarm clouded her face, she looked at me without really seeing me. "The baby," she whimpered. "I think it is coming."

I stared at her, not sure what I was supposed to do. She was clinging to the bookshelf. I pulled at a long strand of hair. It felt good, the slight tingle of pain in my scalp reminding me *I am still here, I am not dead or disappeared.*

"Go, get the phone, Varsha," Suman said, climbing slowly off the ladder and walking wide-legged towards a chair in the middle of the room. "It's the baby. It's coming like an earthquake. We need to call for the ambulance."

"Hello, Soo-man, and how are we today? Baby doing okay, then?" Greta the telephone operator bawled. She always shouts like you're a million miles away and she doesn't actually have a telephone in her hand. She is also the postmistress, and her daughter Leanne Walker who is in my class has a cleft lip and is waiting for an operation to make her beautiful.

"Greta, I need the ambulance immediately," Suman said. "The baby is coming."

"Oh dear!" Greta boomed. "Can you hang on a bit longer, darling? The ambulance and the fire engine are both out there in the mountains, accident on the highway."

Suman mooed again, shaking her head, handing me the phone, say no, can't wait, want it now, coming, the baby is coming.

"Well then, well then, all I can do is give them a call and let them know. Is there someone else at home with you? Where's the big guy, gone to work, eh?" It's a small town, everybody knows everybody else, nothing surprising about that.

Yes, Papa is at work, yes, I'm at home with her, and Akka, but nobody else. I'm too young and my grandmother is too old. How about a friend, then, anyone close by who can help? Surely there's somebody who can help, small towns are full of helpful folks. Just hold on.

Call, call Mrs. Cooper, Varsha, hurry, hurry, hurry, Suman howled, and from her room where she was stuck in her chair my old grandmother warbled high like a bird with a sore throat—*What is it? Is there something wrong?*

Mrs. Cooper showed up after twenty minutes even though she lived only about five minutes away by car, because it took her time to climb into her boots and her jacket and her toque and her gloves, she said, and it took her time to find the car keys and the house keys, and because nobody had cleared the snow from the road leading to our house she'd had to drive super slowly. Ours are the only two homes on that road and every winter, by this time, there is so much snow that it takes four times longer to get anywhere. Akka always said if it wasn't for Mrs. Cooper's two sons who used to come down twice a month to check up on her, or Nick's dad Joe Hutch, who does it once in a while because he's Papa's school friend, that road would be thigh-deep in snow in winter, and no one would ever find us till thaw time came and if it wasn't for them, bless-them-with-a-hundred-dutiful-sons-and-one-loving-daughter-each, we'd be trapped inside our house, buried in snow, frozen and compressed over the winter into flattened versions of ourselves, we would freeze and become snow crystals on our own windows.

Mrs. Cooper limped in, helped Suman into the back seat of her tiny car, panting from the effort, and cried, "Hold on there, honey. We'll get you to the hospital in no time."

I refused to stay behind with Akka—what if my new mother snuck away with the new baby while I waited at home? What *if*? So I too got loaded into the car and Akka was left behind with the phone in her right hand, and her glasses looped around her neck so she could see what she was dialing, just in case she needed to phone somebody all of a sudden, in case she was dying, and she said she was okay and we'd better leave, looks like Suman is about to have her baby NOW. I fixed my grandmother's image inside my head, so she would look exactly the same as she did at that moment, black eyes snapping with life, even if she were to die before we returned. Who knows what a dead person looks like anyway? I've still never seen one. Not even Mom. Do they look like puddles of grey water, for isn't it true that the human body is made up mostly of water? Will Akka look like a brown leaf blown down by the wind? Or will she be just a sad thing like the cat that

Nick Hutch killed by accident with his daisy gun—eyes
shut and mouth open?

"Buckle up, everyone!" shouted Mrs. Cooper. She
climbed into the driver's seat, her smoker's lungs whining
protest with each breath she took, and drove as fast as
she could, which was not very fast because of the snow,
but soon Suman was screaming and begging her to stop,
stop, please stop, the baby is coming. I will make a mess
of your car seat. Please stop. We'd travelled only as far as
Mrs. Cooper's house, so there was nothing to do but turn
into the gate and stop. Mrs. Cooper trundled around to
Suman's side of the car to help her out, but she slipped
out of her seat, half in and half out of the car door, her sari
ruched up around her waist, her soft brown skin turning
blue with cold. I was out too, wide-eyed and shocked,
watching my brother blooming like a hairy flower in the
gasping darkness of the place between Suman's legs, a
swamp of blood spreading about her on the white snow,
and the smell, the stink of new life, and then my newborn
brother screaming from his first encounter with the frozen
world. Mrs. Cooper rushed in and out of her house, dragging a rug from her living room, blankets, boiling water,
scissors, cloth rags, and I stood and watched unnoticed,
chewing a strand of my hair, shivering from cold and fear.
Mine, I thought. *My* brother.

When Suman and the baby returned from the hospital,
I helped her bathe him, held out the towels to dry him,
brought lotions to make him moist and soft and sweet as

fresh butter, held his chubby feet in the air while she changed his diapers, tickled his belly and combed his hair with the soft brush that had once been mine. She put a dot of black kohl on his thigh, like a giant mole on his pallid skin, to keep away the evil eye, and a dot of it on my head, deep inside my hair where it could not be seen by the kids at school.

The months after Hemant's birth were good ones. Suman lost that panicked look in her eyes that terrified me so much, and she stopped crying in Akka's room. For a while Papa smiled and cooed at the baby and made special things for Suman to eat, and bought us expensive presents to show how much he loved us. For a while it was okay and for a while we were the happiest family in the world. But I felt like we were all holding our breaths as hard as we could and pretty soon we'd just have to let go. Pretty soon Suman or I would say or do something that would make Papa mad, and everything would be back to the way it always was.

Suman

In the beginning, I liked Vikram, was curious about him, and flattered that he wanted to marry me. But that was all. What I imagined as "love" did not enter the equation. When he first touched me on our wedding night, I felt only nervousness and a bit of nausea at the thought of lying naked with a stranger. And afterwards, when he held me close, murmuring in my ear words that I was too embarrassed to hear, my legs sticky with our fluids, all I thought about was how soon I could rush to the bathroom and wash it all off. There were none of those feelings of ecstasy that the poets and novelists write about. Were those men writing about how they felt when they made love to a woman? Were men more susceptible to ecstasy? I had no idea. Madhu Kaki had been my sole source of information, and not a very reliable one. I had asked her about how I should feel on the first night of my marriage and she had said quite confidently that I should feel as any bride should.

"And what is that feeling?" I had insisted.

"Why, a deep respect for your husband, my dear, what else?"

"What about love? What if I feel respect but no love?"

"If you respect him, how can you not love him too?" Madhu Kaki had asked.

"I respect the temple priest," I said, "but I don't love him. Should I?"

"What a thing to say! Love Shripad Acharya indeed! Why, he is older than your grandfather might have been if he was alive! And if he had heard you talking this way, he would have died of shock! Chhee!" Madhu Kaki wagged her hand at me and said, "What an odd creature you are! I am sure you will get along very well with your mother-in-law. You two can sit in Canada and spend your time quizzing each other about silly things like love and all. I will thank you to leave me alone!"

I asked her again, the morning of my wedding, beset with doubts. "I don't think I love him, Madhu Kaki," I whispered as my aunt hovered about me, turning me into a bride.

"It will come, this love that you keep talking about," Madhu Kaki assured me, fat chin set in certainty, her arms jiggling as she rubbed turmeric and sandal paste on my arms to make my skin golden and fragrant.

"What if it doesn't?"

"It will, girl, stop questioning me. Look at me and your uncle—I had not even set eyes on him before I married him, and then I felt only love for him afterwards."

"Why?" I persisted.

"What kind of question is that?" Madhu Kaki had been genuinely puzzled. In her innocent, simple world marriage was a prerequisite for love and you fell in love with nobody but the person you married. There were no second chances, mistakes were to be tucked away inside a cupboard smelling of mothballs and sandalwood and regret, and commitments were to be honoured until death. "Your husband will take care of you like your father did, so naturally you have to love him for it."

Could you love somebody out of a sense of obligation? I wondered. Could you love a man simply because you were married to him? No, I know that now. For my aunt, though, the heart was like one of the third-grade pupils whom I tutored—easy to discipline, easy to control.

After the wedding, we went to Mercara to spend a week before my new husband returned to Canada. On the last day of our stay, there was a small incident that unnerved me. He had gone back to our room to get a shawl for me since it was a little chilly, and as I waited in the lobby of the shabby old hotel a young man carrying some suitcases bumped into me. It was an accident. He stopped to apologize and I said, "It's okay." I might have smiled, I don't remember. The next thing I knew, Vikram was there beside us, furious, his eyes violent. He grabbed my arm and dragged me away, asking repeatedly, "Who is he? Where did you meet him?"

And I stammered, wondering whether he had lost his

mind, whether I was stuck in a nightmare, "I don't know who he is, I don't know, I promise."

"What's his name? Don't lie, I know you are lying, you bitch, you're planning to leave me I know!" Vikram was yelling now and people were looking at us and I was crying and thinking, I am married to a crazy person, what am I to do, what am I to do?

We stayed in our room the rest of the evening, me weeping and Vikram pacing the room, and then suddenly, as if it had all indeed been a bad dream, he gathered me in his arms and stroked my hair and buried his face in my neck and whispered, "Don't cry, don't cry, I can't bear to see you crying like this."

Six months later, pushing my luggage trolley into the arrival lounge at the small Merrit's Point airport, I was reminded of this incident. Vikram was waiting for me, bearing a lovely, large bouquet of flowers. A young woman dashed past and flung herself into the arms of a man in a red checked shirt. They looked so happy that I couldn't help smiling. Another man, middle-aged, walking alongside, caught my glance and smiled too—a brief, motiveless sharing of amusement. I felt Vikram's eyes on me and turned away from the hugging couple and the middle-aged man. He was frowning now, holding the bouquet against the side of his leg like a tennis bat.

"Were you waiting long?" I asked nervously.

He turned away and began to walk very fast, leaving me to run behind him, pushing my laden trolley with difficulty.

I caught at his sleeve and stopped him. "Is something wrong?"

He paused to throw the bouquet into a garbage bin. "Why were you smiling at that man?" he asked.

"I wasn't smiling at anybody," I protested.

"Don't play the innocent with me," he said. We had reached a blue car. "I saw you. Did you meet him in the plane?" He wrenched open the trunk and loaded my bags.

I couldn't speak for a few moments and then I said, "I have never seen him before in my life. Why don't you trust me?"

"Why were you smiling at him, then? Do you make it a habit to smile at strange men?" he asked.

He opened the car door, got in, turned the ignition key, and the car roared to life. I went to open the door on my side but he started to back out of the parking spot, so that I had to jump aside. I stood there like a fool, teeth chattering, eyes and nose watering from the cold, while he accelerated away down the lot.

Was he mad? Suddenly I wondered: had his first wife really died in an accident, or was there something more sinister about it? I couldn't believe that he was going to leave me here, all alone, in the freezing parking lot of a strange town in an unknown country. I didn't even have a change of clothing, nothing warmer than the sweater and shawl that I was wearing, and in my handbag was ten dollars—all the money the Indian government allowed a traveller to take out of the country then. In rupees that was a lot of money, but I knew it was not enough for more than a meal or two here. But I hadn't even considered the possibility that I might find myself in a situation where I would need more money than that.

I tried to staunch the flow of panic and drew a deep breath. I had Vikram's address. I would ask somebody at the airport how I could get to his house. I hoped it would cost no more than ten dollars. Once there, I would meet his mother—a woman would be sympathetic to my plight, she would scold her son for making such baseless accusations, and then it would all be fine, it would, it *had* to be. I couldn't fly back to India. I had no ticket. Besides, it would be a shameful thing to do. People would talk. It would hurt my father. I knew nobody else in this country I could turn to for help. For the first time in my life, I felt overwhelming fear, complete loneliness.

There was a scream of tires and the car was back, once again barely missing me as I stood there. Did the man want to kill me? He leaned over and opened the door. "What are you standing there for? Waiting for your boyfriend? Get in!"

As we started off I made an attempt at conversation. "Have you been well?"

"Yes," he said. "Who was that man, you still haven't told me."

I felt tears rising. This was certainly not the kind of reception I had imagined. I looked down, fiddling with my bangles, hoping he would not notice that I was crying. "Nobody," I said. "I don't know anybody here. I just smiled because he smiled, that's all. It meant nothing, may god strike me dead if I am lying."

He didn't say anything for a few minutes and then, in one of those abrupt changes of tone and mood that I have spent the last eight years trying to get used to, he looked at me as if he was seeing me for the first time and asked in a kind voice, "So, was it a tiring journey? Would you like to stop somewhere and eat before we go home to my mother and daughter? Are you hungry?" He grinned like an excited boy, and baffled as I was by this sudden switch in his temper, I smiled back, glad that whatever had gone wrong had turned right mysteriously. I didn't want to question the shift then, I was grateful that he was smiling at me. I even loved him for a brief moment for smiling at me and asking after my comfort. Like a pariah dog that will follow, with tail-wagging adoration, any friendly person who clicks a finger at it.

For a while on that drive to my new home Vikram was chatty and charming. He pointed out mountain ranges as we drove farther north, closer and higher than anything I had ever seen. Only an occasional car passed us. I thought it was beautiful—that fresh air, the soaring mountains, the dark green of the trees. I forgot the strange cruelty that he had displayed only a short time before.

"This is how it must be like driving through the Himalayas," I said impulsively.

Vikram frowned at me. "The Himalayas are much higher, and you can't drive through them like this. Even my five-year-old daughter knows that."

"I'm sorry," I said. "I don't know much, I haven't been anywhere."

That was the beginning of my slide into irrelevance, I think—that admission of ignorance, of stupidity. Sometimes I think back on that morning and use that conversation to lash myself, like one of those priests in stone-walled monasteries who whip themselves bloody so that they can drive the demons out of their souls. My demon—a demon that I had not known lived within me—was my willingness to stay and take it. I stayed for many muddled reasons: fear of this unknown world mostly, lack of money, and because I feared the shame of returning, of dishonouring my father if I left my marriage.

"Marriage is not about getting together," my Appa had said the day before my wedding. "It is about staying together." He had stayed with my mother. Stayed through health and in sickness, and even after she was dead he had stayed true to her memory. I wanted to be as true a spouse as my beloved father had been. So I stayed even though the temptation to run was always there like a strong pulse just beneath my skin. For the last eight years I have tried to do all that he asked me to without a complaint, have looked after him, his child and his mother, tolerated his sudden rages which tear across our lives as frequently and viciously as winter storms. And they were my fault, he would say in the lull that always followed, his face wet with tears, his hands trembling as they roamed over me as if to make sure his words and his blows had not erased me from the face of the earth, crushed me into a dusty nothing.

"Why do you . . . why do you make me say these things?" he would moan. "How many times have I said, don't make me say these things? It hurts me, don't you see?"

In the early years, when I still had some sense of myself, I would feel indignant. *He* was hurt? What about me? But I was still so unsure how I was supposed to deal with him or our relationship. So I made silence my best defence against Vikram's jealous rages, his debilitating meanness, and as the years passed, my own silence has crushed me further. How can it not be to some extent my fault, stupid annoying woman that I have become?

Once, a long time ago, when I was a girl full of hope, some tourists had photographed me in my home town. That hope has leaked out of me now. I think of the photograph often and wish I had a copy so that I might look at it and remember who I was. I wish I could run back to that bright-eyed time, that moment when a different future seemed possible.

Then my son was born, and for a while I thought— an old-fashioned idea—that he would make things better between us, that a child is a strong link between husband and wife, that Vikram would now have proof of my devotion, understand my willingness to stay, that this was my home now, that he would soften. When you are unhappy, you use any little thread, imagined or otherwise, to fabricate an entire quilt to comfort you.

My son arrived before his time, out in the open,

sliding into the snow, right in front of Mrs. Cooper's front door.

I named him Hemant for winter, the season in which he was born. It was to be his talisman against that season and all its attendant demons, a vaccine, like that administered for polio, injected into his body to trigger immunity against the illness called winter that afflicts this land every year.

Despite my own feelings, though, my boy grew to love the wretched season. I wonder if his name allows him into its mysteries, turning it from talisman into a magic sesame of a word, opening doors that lead to untold treasures. Hem sees beauty where I see only misery, he is at home in this wintry world whereas I forever remain a stranger to it. He is always rash-marked and itching and whining through the brief, drenching heat of summer, sniffing, sneezing, wheezing, allergic to everything through spring and autumn, turning red and healthy and energetic only as the days draw close and dark and the sky turns bleak. For some reason, even though this was why I gave him this name, I feel profoundly betrayed by his fondness for the season.

"The snow fell into your eyes," I say accusingly, as if Hem somehow colluded with the weather and made it snow on the day of his birth. "It bewitched you, blinded you to this cold."

And when I am in a worse mood because of the numbing, long winter days that I could never have imagined in Madras, I insist that the snow bhooth flew into his soul on that day despite my best precautions.

"Then why did you name me after it?" Hemant demanded once. "Because you hate me as much as you hate the cold?"

"Hate you? Don't be silly," I said. "You are more to me than my own life. I named you and now you love winter—isn't that the magic of a naming?"

My own naming too had a magic attached to it, but it must have been twisted into bad luck by mischievous spirits. My mother bestowed it on me, and in the worst moments of my life I try to hear the soft whisper of her loving voice in my ear. Suman, she would say, my little blossom. Su-man—meaning flower, beloved only off-spring. Yes, I was a beloved daughter. No one ever hit me, I was not slapped or pinched or punched; nobody ever raised their voice or flung foul names at me if I made a mistake; nobody accused me of being a fool. If I did some-thing wrong, my Appa gently pointed out the problem to me, patted me on the head, told me not to do it again, and forgave me instantly.

"Next time you will do it the right way," he would say mildly, and I, always anxious to please, would make sure I did.

Years later, when I think about those loving times, I find myself wishing perversely that I had been shouted at and beaten, because that way at least I would have learned how to dodge and run, I would have turned as tough as a slipper that has travelled on mean roads. I might even have learned to hit back.

Part Two

ANU AND SUMAN

Anu's Notebook

June 1, 1979. I am here! And it is all I hoped for. Drove through the mountains for a few hours loving the fresh air blowing through my partially open window. A sign informed me that I was approaching Merrit's Point, and within a few minutes the town centre appeared, heralded by a brief line of lamp-posts bedecked with flower baskets. I drove past a few small shops, a grocery store, a café, a church—and then it was finished— before I knew it I was on the highway again. I pressed down on the accelerator, pushing my rattling old car to greater feats of strength and daring, hurtled past darkly wooded patches loud with the chirr-chirring of cicadas and emerged into blinding sunlight. To the right of me the road hugged cliffs composed of scarred rock the colour of sunsets, to the left were fields of undulating green. In the distance the mountains— lavender and blue shading into gloomy purple and navy, smoke and carbon. Imperious, watchful. The jagged peaks still topped with snow.

I arrived at a T-junction and turned off the highway into Fir Tree Lane, a bit of a misnomer, I discovered, since there was not a single tree on it. It was a bald and ragged little lane, pitted and stony. I winced as my poor car bumped and ground and rattled over it, wheezing in exhaustion all the way.

A giant lake shimmered up suddenly, dark green with silver flecks where the sun caught on ripples. I passed a shuttered house, surrounded by weeds, a long stretch of broken-down fencing, and then I was at a gate with an incongruously ornate mailbox painted an iridescent green. My car rattled a few more times, sighed, shuddered and finally collapsed. I cursed aloud, climbed out and surveyed the emptiness stretching out all around me. A longish driveway curled away from the gate and ended at the Dharma house, which crouched low against the ground.

The earth sprawled warm and inviting as a lover beneath the sun. Somewhere an insect made a piercing call, like the high-pitched whine of telephone wires in my brother's backyard in summer. A bee made straight for my face and I whacked furiously at the air, all my city-girl fears rising up—what if I was allergic to bee stings? I wished I had brought bug repellent with me. And antihistamines. And mosquito nets, and spears, and guns, and other things to protect me from this fearsome emptiness, this silence. Then I felt ridiculous. I had come here for the silence and the emptiness and now, within a few minutes, I was ready to run away.

Closer to the house, the scenery changed. A wild-looking garden rose up from the ground, with patches of yellow, pink, purple spreading out haphazardly in all directions. There was a shaggy clump of mock-orange shrubs in full flower, soaking the air with their fragrance. A giant peony, collapsed under the weight of massive magenta flowers, looked like a supplicant in a flouncy skirt praying on her knees.

A woman appeared from around the corner of the house and waved. She was wearing a sari—an incongruous sight in this landscape. I waved back, suddenly glad I was here, surrounded by all this untamed beauty, this quiet, about to meet a woman in a sari.

Suman

I remember when Anu arrived on a warm day in the beginning of summer. Winter was finally over, so my spirits had risen as a result. It was early in the afternoon. I was in the yard at the side of the house, hanging out the washing. I heard the low, uneven drone of a car as it approached the house and then a stutter and silence. A car door slammed. I realized it was probably our new tenant, Anu Krishnan—we had been expecting her earlier that day—though I wondered why she had stopped so far from the house.

It was Vikram's idea to rent out the back-house. His hours were being cut at work, the company was bleeding money and might even close. Someone, maybe Joe Hutch, suggested that renting out the small cottage behind our house would bring in some extra money. I couldn't imagine who would want to leave a bustling life in the city to stay in Merrit's Point, but to my surprise Vikram had at least seven inquiries. People always want to run away from what they have, I suppose. Anu Krishnan said she had been Vikram's classmate at college, although he couldn't remember her at all, and when a common friend told her about his advertisement in their alumni paper she decided to rent it for an entire year. She had paid us for six months in advance as an assurance that she would stay. I envied the woman her control over her life, her money, her future. It seemed she made the decisions, there was nobody she needed to consult. What would she make of me? I must be everything she wasn't.

I could see the roof of the car glinting in the sun, beside our mailbox painted a bright green by Varsha and Hemant. They change the colour every year depending on Varsha's current colour obsession. Hemant goes along with whatever she decrees. It bothers me some-times, how much control my stepdaughter has over my son. Hemant told me once that he belonged to his sister because she saw him first. I don't know what he meant, though he's an imaginative little boy, given to strange thoughts. Besides, I am an only child, so I don't really understand the pacts that siblings make, their secret world which excludes all adults.

I suppose I should be pleased that Varsha is so close to him. I am fond of her—but I am not entirely comfort-able in her presence. She doesn't resent me, I don't think she ever has, and she's ever eager to please. But she always seems to be watching me—I can feel those large black eyes all the time, even when she isn't in the same room. When she was younger she would be glued to me, and on weekends, when she was home, I couldn't leave the house for even a moment without her following me or calling for me.

"Mama?" she used to shout, her voice panicky. "Mama? Where are you? Where are you?"

And what a fuss she would create over going to school! "Don't want to go today," she whined every morning. Or: "I feel sick." She would vomit out her cereal to prove she was ill. At school, her teachers said she fidgeted and fought with other children, tilted her chair back so far that it crashed over, and then she would cry that she had a headache from the fall, was feeling dizzy, needed to go home. The teachers complained to me—or anyway they complained to Vikram—but I was as helpless as they were—she was not my child and I had little idea how to handle her. But when I asked Vikram what to do about her, he said in that cold, frightening voice he uses with me, "You are her mother, you have to deal with it. That's why you are here."

She will grow out of it, I told myself, trying hard to be a mother to the girl whose strange ways I could not understand. Her mother died, she is so young, she must still be feeling so insecure about it—as if that explained everything. And perhaps it did. I remembered how alone I had felt when my mother died. And how glad I had felt to have my Madhu Kaki. Perhaps the teachers thought so too. I think they worked hard to be kind to Varsha even though she must have tried their patience as thoroughly as she did mine. If I scolded her, she would complain to her father, who would in turn shout at me for ill-treating her. Or he would smack her instead, depending on his mood.

Then one day I had had all that I could take from her and with some of my old spirit told her firmly that if she did not stop her nonsense immediately, I would go away. "You will not find me waiting for you at the bus stop, you will not find me at home," I threatened. She turned white, the blood draining from her little face.

"Don't you dare go away from us," she shouted at me. "If you do, I will kill you, I promise, Mama, I will, I will."

I laughed. "How can you kill me if I am already gone, Varsha?" I asked her, making her even more enraged.

"I will kill you before you go," she said fiercely. I looked at her grim, tense face and was almost willing to believe her.

"What a thing to say, Varsha!" I was startled by her expression—so adult and a bit frightening, I have to admit. "If you kill me, you will still not have me here. I will be gone, so don't say such silly things."

"I'll have your photograph on the wall next to my grandpa and we will still be a family," she said.

I stared at my stepdaughter, baffled by her bizarre reasoning, which allowed her to think that a dead stepmother was better than one who had abandoned her. I thought it was Vikram's fault. He had twisted the child's mind. Then she smiled at me, radiantly, like the sun breaking through cloud gloom, and running to me, wrapped her arms around my legs so my momentary unease disappeared. A childish outburst, I told myself, nothing more, I should be glad she cannot bear the thought of a life without me, that she has actually come to love me.

After that, though, Varsha stopped misbehaving. Her tantrums ceased, and except for her insistence on following me around—which is, after all, quite harmless—she is the perfect child.

The woman held out her hand and smiled at me. "Hello! I am Anu Krishnan. And you must be Mrs. Dharma?"

"Yes, but please to call me Suman." I was suddenly conscious of my pronounced Indian accent which I have never managed to lose despite Vikram's best efforts. *Why do you insist on talking like a village idiot? Make an effort, if you please.*

She had a chipped front tooth, I noticed. Olive skin, sweep of hair falling across a wide forehead, brown eyes, not much taller than me. She was smartly dressed in a summery shirt and tight jeans and had an air of confident strength about her.

I nodded towards her car. "Why did you leave that there? You can bring it in."

"The wretched thing broke down. Probably ran out of gas. I suppose it is safe to leave it there? My bags are in the trunk."

"Oh yes." I nodded reassuringly. "Nobody comes here, so don't worry."

"Then I'll go back when it's a little cooler and get my things."

"Vikram will help you." I prayed that he wouldn't be

angry with me for offering on his behalf. Even after eight years with him, I feel on shifting sands, fearful of his reactions to everything, anything.

We walked towards the house in silence and then she turned and smiled happily at me. "This is so lovely."

She was very pretty, I realized. Her thick short hair was beautifully cut. Her skin glowed with health, her mouth shiny with a pale-coloured lipstick. I wondered what it was like to be her.

"I hope it will not be too boring for you," I said self-consciously.

"Oh no! Just what I need. No distractions, oodles of space, and all this silence. I already feel I could live here forever. Perfect—complete isolation."

I smiled politely. "You are taking some leave from work?" I asked. Was it possible to take an entire year off?

"I resigned. I need to think about where I am going. And to vegetate a bit. If it doesn't work out, I can always pick up where I left off."

Vegetate. What an odd word. Why would anyone wish to turn into a vegetable, I thought, be stuck in one place until somebody pulls you out or chops you up for the cooking pot? Although it's true the woman couldn't have found a better place in which to become a rooted vegetable—in Merrit's Point, or Jehannum as Akka calls this town—the Urdu word for Hell, a place so deep that if a stone were to be thrown in, it would travel for seventy years to reach the bottom, with walls so thick it would take the equal of forty long years to cut through them.

"I am hoping to work on some stories," Anu continued. "And this is the perfect place for it. No interruptions, nobody I know, nothing going on that I want to be a part of. Heaven!"

"That must be a nice thing to do," I said vaguely. "What kind of stories? I mean, what will you write about?"

"I don't know yet." She shrugged. "That's why I am here. To find material."

"Here?" I laughed. "You think you will find a story in Merrit's Point? *Nothing* happens here."

"You *live* here, so it's harder to recognize the stories even if they're standing right in front of you. But I'm an outsider, everything is grist for the mill for me. All that I don't know, or find strange, anything I wonder about, will turn into a story. At least, I hope it will. We'll see."

"What does your family think of this? Your husband? Are you married? Children?" I had not seen any markers of marriage—no rings, necklaces, bangles, nothing. But Anu was a Westerner, she had grown up here, in this country, not India, even if her ancestors came from there. I would discover that her signs and symbols were different, that she didn't believe in any of those markers.

"Hah, the great Indian questions. I got asked them all the time when I went to India!" Anu gave a small, sarcastic laugh. "I was married for a year and a half but am not any longer, he was a jerk, and if you asked him, he'd tell you I was a bitch. No children, thank goodness, not that I have anything against them. I couldn't be bothered with the diapers and breastfeeding and puking and all that mothering stuff. I have one brother who doesn't approve of me, but to his credit he doesn't stop me from spoiling his kids—two boys who love and adore Aunty Anu. My mother is very old and kind of senile and in a nursing home. My father died a couple of years ago. I am forty-three years of age, and not looking for attachments for the time being. And yes, I admit, I must be crazy to have left a job with a fabulous salary, but I've always dreamed of writing stories, and so here I am, your tenant, hoping to have a book at the end of her stay. Or at least a draft." She stopped, drew a deep breath, raised an eyebrow at me and said, "Anything else?"

"So sorry, I didn't mean to offend you," I stammered, feeling foolish, feeling like I do when I say something that annoys Vikram, makes him look at me as if I am ridiculous.

"No, no, I'm not offended at all!" Anu stopped in her tracks and caught my arm. "Why should I be? *I* apologize for sounding like I did. It's just that, for a moment there, I thought I was back in India, all those ammas and aunties checking me out as a prospective bride. You know what I mean, right?"

I smiled and nodded. "Yes, I do. They grab you by the chin and turn your face this way and that, ask you all kinds of things about private matters, as if you are for sale or something. They used to do that to me all the time." And then Vikram came along, asked nothing, and like a fool I married him. Of course I don't say this to the bright, sparkling woman who has arrived at our door.

"Checking to see if you have grown an extra ear or are hiding a mole." Anu chuckled. "So, tell me, Suman, where in India do you come from? Village, tribe, caste, sub-caste, etc, etc."

"I am from Madras, down south, near the sea." I was silent for a few minutes, thinking of a narrow gully, the shadow of an ancient temple that was still, always, super-imposed on my dreams. "And you? You are also hailing from the south, I think?" I couldn't catch the little Indianism before it slipped out of my mouth. "I mean, you come from the south? From your name it seems so."

"Hailing from is much more interesting, I think," Anu said. "I hail from Tamil Nadu on my father's side and Bengal on my mother's. They met at university and I am told it was love at first sight. I think my poor mother died a little bit when my father did and she's gone rapidly downhill since then. Now she hardly knows who we are. She is waiting to end."

"I am sorry to hear that," I said. "It must be very dif-ficult for you."

We had stopped at the front door. "Would you like to come in and have some juice or cold water? Then I can take you to the back-house."

"Juice would be lovely, thanks." Anu trailed after me into the kitchen. She peered out of the window at the green wilderness outside. "No kitchen garden?"

"We had a very nice one before. My mother-in-law, you know. She has green fingers, everything she put in the ground grew. Such huge zucchini and tomatoes—even after squirrels and the birds got their share, we had so much. I tried to keep it going for a while, but I am not very good at it. Now I have given up. Only some herbs and chilies I plant."

"Does your mother-in-law live here with you?"

"Yes, she is old, and can't move. She had a stroke a few years ago. But her mind is still very sharp—although after her stroke, sometimes she wanders. Poor thing, she has her good days and bad ones also."

As if she knew we were speaking about her, Akka called out from her room. "Suman, is she here? Our tenant?"

I gave Anu an apologetic look. "She likes company. Is it okay? You will come in and say hello to her? If you don't mind, of course."

"I would love to meet her," Anu said enthusiastically. "I like old people. They have the most amazing stories, the rich material of a long life."

I nodded. This woman was determined to find stories under every stone, it seemed to me.

Akka beamed at us and patted the bed beside her chair. "Come, sit, talk to me. It is a long time since one of Vikram's friends visited."

I excused myself. "I have to hang the clothes, Akka. I left them lying outside in a bundle in the basin."

Akka waved impatiently at me. "Tchah! Sit for two minutes, nothing will happen that hasn't happened already to those sheets." She turned to Anu. "Did I hear you say something about stories? I could tell you plenty."

"In that case, I will be here every day," Anu laughed.

I made for the door. "Oh no! Look at the time! The children must be wondering why I am not there."

"Suman, Varsha is old enough to bring her brother home from the bus stop on her own," Akka said firmly. "For goodness' sake, she's thirteen. I don't know why you need to go every day all the way there and wait. It is not as if there are twenty confusing roads from there to here! Sit. They will be all right without you."

"They will be upset," I insisted. "Hem expects me to be there. And Vikram is particular about it."

"He can stop expecting for one day. And we won't tell Vikram. You spoil those children, give in too much to everything they want. Sit, I say, I will tell them it was my decision." She turned back to Anu. "Now tell me about yourself and why you want to sit in a hut in this Jehannum all summer."

Anu did not complain about anything. Even when she entered our glorified shack—for that is what it really is— she was full of enthusiasm.

"How pretty it looks," she said, noticing the effort I'd taken to turn the place into a home of sorts with colour- ful cushions and good pots and pans, which I'd bought when Vikram took us all to town for our weekly groceries the Saturday before. I even found some ancient fashion magazines inside an unused cupboard, which I assume belonged to Vikram's first wife.

Anu was like that—never failed to say something

kind about everything I did. In those warm summer months she would come over often, to chat or tease Akka, her voice bright and happy as she talked, or potter around in the back garden while I cooked in the kitchen. At first we never told Vikram about her visits—neither Akka nor I—we had a pact of silence about certain things. I don't know why Akka kept quiet, but I did because I didn't know how Vikram would react. He might have objected. It wasn't included in her rental contract, he might have said, to be entertained by her landlady. And somehow Anu had understood that she was not to mention her visits either. I had worried about Varsha reporting to her father, the way she is given to doing, to get a pat on the head from him, his approval. We all do it. Anything to avoid his anger. All of us carrying tales to him about each other, falling over ourselves to be in his good books, I as childish as my stepdaughter.

In the end it was Akka who came up with the idea of telling Vikram, if he asked, that she was responsible for Anu's visits in the afternoon. "I'll tell him I don't feel very safe alone in the house when you go off to fetch the children," my mother-in-law said, patting my arm one morning when I was helping her with her bath. "I'll say it is comforting to have Anu here with me. He won't object to that, you'll see." By the time the summer holidays began, everyone had gotten used to Anu's frequent presence in the house, taking tea with Akka. In any case, even before that it never came up, and now it does not matter. Akka is in hospital, tethered to her bed by intravenous tubes, lost inside the ruined corridors of her brain, waiting for death which hovers over her, fills her lungs with rattling stones, her eyes with grey mist.

And Anu is gone.

Anu's Notebook

June 10. The Dharma house is truly isolated. The only inhabited building for miles around. The neighbour's place, the abandoned-looking structure I passed on my way down Fir Tree Lane, has been lying vacant since its owner's departure a few years ago. Suman is worried, I think, that the wilder local kids from Merrit's Point come out to smoke and drink there—there are no doubt some tough kids in this area.

My cottage, or back-house as the Dharmas call it, is a small, bare studio with windows on one wall, a kitchenette with an ancient stove and a stained sink, a bathroom with an old-fashioned claw-footed tub, and a wooden table where I work. Fanning out in all directions around it are trees and shrubs and creeping undergrowth creating a cool, greenish-gold light which I find soothing. Suman tells me there is nothing beyond the surrounding trees except more of the same. I intend to explore farther as soon as possible.

This morning I woke early, headed out for a walk down that bald lane and stopped by the lake. The dark green surface of the water was stretched tight, like skin on a drum. Insects hummed up in black swarms from the jumble of vegetation rimming it. *Plip-plop*—a fish or a frog leapt out of the water, was suspended in light for a moment, a scaly, shimmering angel, and fell back in. Rings of water pulsed away from that small movement and I expected a northern naiad to rise out dramatically.

In the afternoon I bumped into the children Varsha and Hemant.

"Hello, how are you?" The girl is always polite.

"I'm fine, thanks," I replied. "I spent the morning beside your lake. It's lovely."

"It's not our lake," the girl said.

"There are dead bodies in it," the boy added.

What an imagination! "How do you know? Have you seen any?" I asked.

The child gave me a serious look. "Varsha said."

Even in the short time I've been here—and I don't see the kids that often—I've discovered it is Hemant's favourite response to most questions. *Varsha said.* The two of them are stuck to each other like halves of a clamshell.

The lane, the lake, the trees and the mountains, the abandoned house, the main road—that pretty much defines our immediate surroundings. I am not complaining. This is what I wanted: isolation, time to think and write, silence. The silence, especially, is astonishing. I can hear my own breath even in the middle of the morning. Tonight I stood outside and stared up at the vastness of the night sky with stars spilling in grand chaos in every direction, so close I feel I can reach out and pluck them like jewelled fruit. I imagine Vikram's father, Mr. J.K. Dharma, who built this house, standing here much as I did, squinting up at the sky, his head cocked as he listened for sounds and hearing only the wind in the brooding darkness of the trees and the bullfrogs striking up their deep contrapuntal croaking. Perhaps the silence filled him with contentment. In India he must have grown up in a house packed with children and relatives, in a city crowded with sounds, and longed to get away from it all. I could make up anything about this unknown, unknowable man and it could be true. In a landscape such as this one, wiped clean at regular intervals by the snow, histories are surely re-created a hundred times over, memories minted anew, and nobody minds or cares.

June 15. I have set up a schedule of sorts for my day, starting with a walk in the morning, sometimes catching up with Suman and the children on their way to the bus stop at the T-junction where the highway meets Fir Tree Lane. Then I settle down at my desk to write for three or four hours, regardless of whether the creative juices are flowing or not, break for lunch, sit down again at the desk, then take a break for tea with the Dharma women. If Akka is feeling well and Suman isn't too busy. Without the discipline, I might not get any writing done at all! A nap, some more work or not, and then it's time for bed.

Now my car is back from the service station, I sometimes drive into Merrit's Point for a coffee and groceries.
The small town has a tentative, ephemeral quality to it, as
if it knows in its bones that the mountains clambering
over each other to peer down at it from all sides will
someday slide down and obliterate it, or that winter one
year in the near future will never leave and we will be
conquered by snow at last.

A long time ago it was a thriving community, I'm told,
famous for its copper mines. The tiny local library has
some good photographs of the founder, Alfie Merrit.
The pleasant young librarian, Laura, told me that according to legend, Alfie thought he was on the trail of gold.
He hacked through wild roses and brambles that climbed
in thorny tangles along the edges of pine forests, crossed
jewelled lakes and nameless mountains, followed by a few
other fools all dreaming of great wealth. There was no
gold, but they found copper, which dried up within ten
years, moved to lumber, which they chopped down faster
than it would grow, and ever since, still waiting for the
earth to regenerate itself and reveal more treasures, the
town has slipped ever deeper into obscurity. Each year,
Laura complained, more and more people, the younger
lot especially, pack their bags and move to busier towns
and cities and never return except for the funerals of the
ones they've left behind. I said I'd noticed that the single
main street that runs through the town is crowded with
grey-haired grannies and grandfathers scooting around in
wheelchairs, or pushing themselves painfully along with

their walkers. And outside of town, abandoned houses dot the empty landscape like dead flies, shuttered windows gazing sightlessly at passersby.

The town is, to be honest, a grey place now, although Mrs. Jellinek, one of its inhabitants, feels otherwise. She seems to be—or thinks she is—the la-di-dah, high-mucky-muck of Merrit's Point. Last Friday, I bumped into her almost as soon as I pulled up in the parking lot of the post office. She was wearing shorts and a T-shirt and looked like a stringy chicken in clothes, I thought meanly, and immediately felt ashamed since she was prancing along quite happily.

"My nephew is coming to visit this afternoon," Mrs. Jellinek said, wrapping bony fingers around my wrist firmly. "He's a big shot in Vancouver, you know. Engaged to Violet Williams—do you know the Williamses?"

I shook my head, mystified. Why on earth would she expect me to know the Williamses! "Also big shots?" I hazarded, since it was obvious that Mrs. J. associates only with that variety.

She opened her eyes wide. "Oh yes, my dear, Very Important People. Very Old Family. Rooted. My nephew is blessed, you know."

"I am sure," I said.

"He is coming here to invest in property." I could see Mrs. J. was climbing onto a favourite hobby horse and was about to start rocking away for all she was worth. "Mark my words, this town has gold written all over it. You better get yourself a piece of the pie, dear." She leaned closer and whispered, "I have some land you might want to consider."

She is not the only colourful character in town; there are a few more. The coffee shop, for example, is run by a vast man named Bradford. He has grey-blond hair receding from his forehead in a C-shaped curve and creeping down the back of his neck like a hairy question mark. He dresses like Elvis Presley and occasionally entertains his customers by singing for them. Rather well, too. He told me quite seriously that he is a reincarnation of Elvis and was offended when I laughed. He is a chatty fellow, full of interesting little tidbits about people and events in the little town, and since his café is the only one that serves half-decent coffee, I always go in when I am there. He has three employees: two girls around seventeen or so and a younger boy, Nick, who helps out on weekends.

Bradford and his three young employees are usually dressed in canary yellow T-shirts and yellow caps with "Badfoods" embroidered across them. He told me the person who did the embroidery got the spelling wrong and gave him a full refund. But Bradford didn't see any reason why he should throw away an otherwise good product and hadn't bothered with a new set of caps and shirts. "I don't give a dog fart about the spelling," he said when I smilingly noted the error. "People don't come here to look at my clothes, ma'am, they come for my coffee."

Unlike Mrs. Jellinek, Bradford doesn't think much of Merrit's Point. He's told me at least four times so far that he is planning to close down shop.

The last time he said that, Cindy, the waitress with the red hair, remarked, "Yeah, right, Bradford! Keep saying it and we might even start believing you!" Then she turned to me and shook her head. "It's all hot air. He ain't going nowhere, take my word for it."

Bradford, like Mrs. J., is clearly an establishment here. Like most of the other inhabitants in this town, they are not leaving—except in their caskets to the local grave-yard, from where they will no doubt emerge as ghouls to bother the living.

"So why don't you sell up and leave if it's so hard for you?" I needled him.

"Who the hell is going to buy me out? Nobody wants to come to this town, do they?"

"Well, Mrs. Jellinek says land values are going through the roof. There will be resorts and condos coming up pretty soon, she says."

"Bollocks! That old nutter knows bugger all. She's trying to unload her land to some idiot, that's all." He gave me a sharp look. "She tried to sell you a piece of it, didn't she? Eh? What did I say?" He grinned. "Old bitch!"

And I couldn't help grinning back.

Suman

It was Vikram's father, Mr. J.K. Dharma, who had come to Merrit's Point first, and his son and grandchildren had no choice after that. In the early days of my life in Merrit's Point, I would stand at the kitchen window washing the dishes, looking out at that wall of dark green beyond the vegetable patch, and wonder what kind of strange man my father-in-law had been to choose this place on earth over all others. When I lay awake in bed after Vikram had raided my unresisting body, I'd make an arrow of my misery and fling it in the direction of Mr. J.K. Dharma. I cursed him for his lunacy in selecting this town to settle in, rather than one of the larger cities such as Vancouver or Toronto, where I was certain I might have found help. I would look up at the large framed photograph of the man hanging on the living room wall, garlanded with plastic flowers strung in a chain, and wonder if he was aware that his choice had ruined my life.

Years before my arrival, Mr. J.K. Dharma had travelled from India to Canada for the same reasons most people of his time did—to get away from sameness, to make money, perhaps also dreaming of an end to irrelevance in a country that had so many people that the loss of thousands every year did not matter much. Apart from this house and a few photographs, my father-in-law left no information about his origins. Across the front page of a diary that smells of mould, he drew his name in careful, cursive ink: *Mr. J.K. Dharma*. What was his first name? Jaishankar? Jagannath? Jaidev? I have never found out. When I asked Akka, the old lady shrugged and quoted a verse in Sanskrit about names having nothing to do with who one really is. And why the insistence on Mr.? The formality of it, as if without that honorific before his neatly parcelled name my husband's father would be undone. On the diary page that followed he had written two brief sentences in the same careful hand: "This is all mine. Silence at last.—J.K. Dharma." It is otherwise empty.

When I first came to this house as a new bride, I, too, was awed and delighted by the amount of space that surrounded me after the noise and bustling crowds of Madras. I helped my mother-in-law in the backyard, where we grew bell peppers and eggplants, tomatoes and beans, zucchini, potatoes, pumpkins, covering everything with chicken wire to prevent marauding creatures from getting our carefully tended produce. It was peaceful out there in the sun, the warm soil loose in my hands, the hum of insects informing me of a busy world that had nothing to do with the fraught one in which I lived. And there was the pleasure the children derived from discovering the first tomato forming on its hairy stalk, pulling out tender carrots even before they were completely ready, the sight of a hummingbird palpitating over bright red bean flowers. Hemant was a toddler then, and Varsha gentler, more innocent.

I remember how Hemant, only three, planted a penny in the soil because his sister had told him to.

"Water it every day," she said seriously. "In two months it will grow into a money-plant ten feet long and you'll be the richest man in Merrit's Point and then you can buy each of us a lovely present."

So he waited for his penny to grow, watering it diligently every day, squatting over the patch waiting for something to pop up, telling me in his high, sweet child's voice about the things he would buy for me and his sister with his harvest of pennies. And it was Varsha who woke early one morning and stuck a long wild creeper that she'd yanked out from the edge of the forest into Hemant's little patch of earth, and scattered pennies around it for her brother to discover.

After Akka damaged her back, I tried to take care of the garden for a while. But it became too much for me to guard against the marauding squirrels and birds, the deer and the raccoons. Now the forest that we held at bay with spade and loppers has crept back to reclaim what it had lost, a green silence in summer and in winter a dormant world under its cover of snow. I used to sing to myself to defeat the silence, I chattered endlessly to Akka, my only companion during the day, and to Varsha after she returned from school. But such is the power of this place that it drove my own voice out of me.

I knew very quickly that I should not stay here. For a while I plotted to escape and, until Hemant was born, I was convinced that I could. Every week I waited until Vikram had left for work after giving me elaborate instructions on all the things that needed to be done around the house that day—

One shirt button to be replaced
Two trousers to be ironed
An entire house to be properly dusted
Laundry
Windows to be cleaned, the third window in the
upstairs spare bedroom on which my husband
had spotted some smudges

—and I would dream of running away.

I had no idea how I would accomplish this since I had no money. Then my passport disappeared. Perhaps Vikram hid it—but I didn't dare ask him. It would only have given him reason to shout at me for my carelessness or stupidity or any of the number of flaws I've developed since I became his wife. I don't possess a driver's licence—he doesn't think I need to drive. So here I am stuck in a world full of borders and boundaries, unable to travel because I can't show proof of my identity to the people who guard the entryways and exits. It is not enough to say, I am Suman, daughter of a beloved man, wife of a hated one. I still need a piece of paper with my photo-graph, stamped by the government of a country. Without that I am nobody other than the wife of a man who is my guardian, my custodian, my prison.

I spent hours wishing myself away from Merrit's Point. I wished I had the courage to run until I reached the highway beyond Merrit's Point that would take me to Vancouver, which shimmered in my imagination like a mirage. I thought of running away all the time, and then one day I gave up that thought too. I can remember the moment when I stopped trying.

Varsha brought home a Russian doll which she had won in an essay competition at school.

"Look, Mama!" she said. She pulled one doll away to reveal another and another and another until she got to the last one, when a tiny black beetle emerged and scuttled across the table, released from captivity after god only knows how long. I screamed and knocked the pile of dolls away. That beetle was me, caught inside the house, inside the town, within the circling mountains.

There is no escape for me from this place.

My father and Madhu Kaki never found out about my unhappiness. I didn't tell them, it was pointless. There was nothing they could have done for me. They didn't have the means to help. Besides, I couldn't contact them without Vikram finding out. I could not telephone long-distance without him knowing when the bills arrived, and when I wrote letters he mailed them for me after reading them first, naturally. "Leave the envelope open, Suman," he would say. "I would like to add a line or two to your dear father."

So I created a lovely tracery of lies for my beloved Appa, warbled on pleasantly about how happy I was, how big my house was, how lucky I was.

Then he died, followed soon after by Madhu Kaki, and there was nowhere for me to run to.

Anu's Notebook

June 20. My cottage is quite far beyond the main house, and the tangle of trees and bushes prevents me from seeing it except at night when the lighted windows wink golden. The family has a routine: Vikram leaves for work first, followed by the children, who are always accompanied by Suman to the bus stop. I don't see why she has to go with them—that girl Varsha is old enough to walk alone with her brother. Other than members of the family, I have seen nobody coming to the house, not even the mailman. It is so quiet and isolated here that I have little trouble convincing myself that we are the only people alive in this town!

Sometimes, wandering around the backyard, looking for a sprig of parsley or coriander which Suman has given me permission to pick, I catch sight of her through the kitchen window busy with morning chores. I imagine her measuring out ingredients, chopping and cutting vegetables, washing the dishes, all with that endearing look of intense concentration that has become familiar to me.

When I say something, she listens with all her might as if I'm god delivering the ultimate truth about life.

She looks very young, even though I know she is thirty-nine years old—another bit of information she handed to me along with the fact that she was already thirty when she got married, that the girl, Varsha, is not her own child, that Hemant was born outside in the snow—a fact that fills her with deep embarrassment even though I tell her the boy now has a good story to tell for the rest of his life—and that Vikram was married before. I heard about the first wife from Carole Mattson. She manages to keep tabs on everybody in our university year—who has got married, who divorced, who had children, moved to Timbuctoo, died, that kind of thing. It was Carole who spotted the ad in the alumni paper for a small cottage for rent up north. When she phoned me in New York, she said she'd also heard Vikram Dharma might be having money problems, that the small lumber mill he worked for as an accountant was laying people off. "Do you remember him?" she asked me. "Kind of stand-offish guy, quiet. Didn't mix much with most of us? Always got great grades. Don't know what Helen saw in him."

I did remember him. Vaguely. A good-looking man. But he obviously couldn't place me, because when I called him and mentioned we were in the same class, he clearly drew a blank. It was such a long time ago, he said, hard to keep track of everybody.

Carole said he'd married Helen Gupta from our Political Science class, whom I did remember—drop-dead gorgeous, busy having a good time, always scrambling to get her assignments done last minute. She, by contrast, was charming and lots of fun.

"She married him and went off to live in a small town up north? Why on earth?" I asked, baffled.

"God knows, but I heard rumours she was already seeing someone else—was going to leave Vikram—but she was in a car crash before that happened. Killed instantly. Sad."

"Did he know she was leaving?" I was curious. I wanted to know more about the man if I was going to be his tenant.

"I don't know. He was devastated by her death, I heard. But not so torn up obviously, since he found himself another wife within the year. You can fill me in on all the details when you take time off from your writing spree—or are you planning to go into hibernation for the next six months?"

A year, I told her, not six months. A whole, blissful year off from my high-octane, frenetic Wall Street life. Write. See if I can do it. Finally. What I've always wanted to do, and if I don't try now I never will.

Most mornings, at around eleven-thirty, Suman arrives at my door, bearing a tray loaded with bowls of food. It's become a habit with her, sneaking to my place with samples of her cooking. I've stopped protesting against such generosity. I understand that the food is an excuse to talk. She's lonely with nobody other than the old lady for company. She never seems to leave the house except to drop off or meet the children at the bus stop every weekday at exactly the same time, or on Saturdays when her husband takes her to the stores in town. The children stay at home then to keep the old lady company. I've hardly seen Vikram yet—he appears to be a controlling sort of guy. His family tiptoe around him like a bunch of mice. I never see anyone visiting them.

She was here again today as usual, fresh in a white and yellow sari, bright against the silent greenery. "Hello?" She peered around the open door. "I can come in? Something for your lunch. I am disturbing you?" She held out a tray covered with a tea cloth.

"Well, I was working..." I started, jumping up to help her with the tray, feeling only slightly guilty about accepting her generosity with such ease, wondering whether there is anything I can do to return the favour.

Her face fell into lines of anxiety. "Sorry! I am sorry to interrupt. I will go now. Bye-bye!" She brushed past me, placed the tray on my crowded table and turned away.

"No, no, please don't leave." I caught her arm and pulled her back. "I was about to take a break anyway. Stay! Shall I make us some tea?"

Suman's face brightened up immediately—she is quite pretty when she smiles. "I will make tea, you see if you like the food I brought for you. Special recipe from my Madhu Kaki."

"No, *you* sit." I pushed her gently into my chair. "You are in my house, as my guest, so *I* get to make the tea. Maybe not as good as the chai you make, but not bad either."

Her forehead creased into the worried frown it so often wears. "Sorry, yes of course it is your house. I am sorry."

"Suman, stop apologizing all the time!" I exclaimed. "You can say anything you want—I won't be upset, I promise."

She gave me a doubtful look, and then lifted the cloth off the tray with a flourish, like a magician, revealing three bowls of food, colourful and fragrant. She looked at me eagerly, a child waiting for praise. "Taste and see if everything is okay?"

I put a spoonful of food from each of the bowls in my mouth and said, honestly, "Mmm, amazing, really, you shouldn't spoil me like this!"

I don't mean it, I'm afraid. Thanks to Suman's daily supply of food, I am saving quite a bit of money as well as eating far better than I deserve or could have imagined. Vikram isn't aware of her generosity, I know. Last Saturday, I bumped into the two of them just as they were heading out on their weekly trip into town. Vikram asked if I had settled in. "If there is anything you require, you can ask my wife."

"I'm fine, thank you," I said. "Suman has been extraordinarily generous already!"

"Oh yes?" Vikram looked at her. "And how has my wife been generous?"

Before I could reply, Suman rushed in. "Nothing, it was really nothing. I only gave her some green chilies she forgot to buy in town. Isn't that so?" She turned. I was startled by her pleading look. I nodded, wondering what was going on.

June 25. I haven't seen Suman today, although I was out for a while by the house, picking some flowers from the unkempt but pretty front garden in which plants have seeded themselves with abandon. It's a mayhem of colour there. At some point in time there was a garden which was loved, obviously—even my untrained eye can pick out domestic favourites such as peonies, roses, day lilies. I assume it was Akka's doing.

June 27. At around noon, a few hours after everybody had left for work or school, Suman was at my door again, bearing a tray of food. She waited, fidgeting, while I tasted the dishes, unable to persuade her to eat with me. I was exclaiming over the delicate procession of flavours when she said in a nervous burst, "Please don't mention to Vikram about this. He might get upset, you know?"

I tried to reassure her quickly. "Suman, you don't need to bring all this food for me. Honestly. And if it gets you in trouble with your husband, all the more reason not to."

But she looked miserable, as if I had criticized her. "You don't like my cooking?" she asked, dismayed.

"No, it's not that. Your food is exquisite—I've never even tasted some of these dishes, and we come from the same part of India! It's just that I don't want any unpleasantness between you and Vikram because of this."

"If he doesn't know, he won't get angry." She threw me a look of childlike cunning. "So if you like what I make, you must not tell him. Or my children. They might tell their father by mistake, especially Hem. He can never keep a secret."

"And your mother-in-law? Akka? She doesn't mind?"

"No, no, she will not let me down, she is good to me."

I can't help wondering about Vikram. He seems to be quite a little tyrant although he's polite and nice enough the few times I've met him so far. He had seemed such an ordinary fellow at university. I suppose you never really know a person until you live with them.

June 29. Alas, no more free gourmet lunches. The summer vacations have begun and the children are home all day now. Suman told me apologetically that she wouldn't be able to come over for a while. She makes up for this by plying me with snacks when I visit Akka. The old lady insists on seeing me almost every day. She likes a good chat and I've made it a habit to visit in the afternoons.

August 13. I decided to take pastries from the bakery in town over for tea—small return for all the meals I've eaten. Hemant was thrilled with the treat and even his odd sister smiled at me. Akka was delighted and gobbled one with groans of pleasure. Suman watched her with an expression of concern and finally protested. "You shouldn't eat such a big piece, Akka, not good for you."

"They might not be good for my stomach, but they make me happy, and at my age that is more important than the health of my body." Akka gave me a naughty look. "Don't listen to a word Suman says, Anu. I can eat anything I want, the doctor told me so."

"No he didn't, she is lying"—laughed Suman—"she will be awake all night complaining of heartburn."

"Come, come, Sumana," Akka said. "Allow me a few last pleasures before I die!"

Suman covered her ears at this and said angrily—if she is capable of anger at all—"Don't talk of dying, Akka, please." She is genuinely fond of the old lady, sees her as some sort of ally in this house, I believe, and can't bear to think of her as an absence.

Part Three

HEMANT AND ANU

Hemant

I am Snowking. I was born outside Mrs. Cooper's house and nearly got eaten by the snow-monster but my mother gave me my name—Hemant—which was my good-luck charm and snatched me away from the jaws of death. Now everybody calls me Hem.

My parents are Suman and Vikram Dharma. They fight a lot. My Papa makes Mama cry every day. Sometimes he pinches her. Varsha says Mama is always looking for her passport to run away from us all. But Varsha says she's hidden it somewhere safe so Mama won't leave us. She says Papa told her a long time ago before I was born that it was her Duty to make sure Mama doesn't go away like her First Mother. She says Mama is delicate and doesn't really know what she's doing and would never be able to survive without us, her family, if she ran away. I don't think Mama is delicate I think she's strong but Varsha says I'm a silly-billy and wouldn't see anything even if it jumped up and bit me on the nose.

Mama has no money except a hundred and two dollars which she hides inside the green and gold sari made of shiny silk given to her by her old aunty Madhu Kaki who looked after her like a mother. The gold in the sari is actually real silver covered with gold. It is a family Heirloom which Varsha will get when she is married. But Varsha says she will never get married and go away and leave me. Mama tells me lots of stories about when she was small like me in India. She says she wants to go back there and live forever and ever and she wants to take me with her. When I tell Varsha, she gets mad and says I don't know anything and shouldn't spread lies and I should shut up. I don't tell lies or make things up. But Varsha can be scary mad even though I love her and she loves me. So I shut up but here is what I remember from what happened last year when I was six. Mama had a dead baby that looked like a fish with hands and no eyes. I am good at remembering things everyone else wants to forget.

It was at night, after Christmas time. It was very cold. If you went out the wind hurt you. Even the moon looked kind of frozen. There were a zillion stars in the sky, holding it tight. It looked like a black sheet over our town. Varsha said the more clear the sky, the more cold it is. Mama and Akka hate our town. Akka says it's a nowhere place. She says it's the armpit of hell fit only for cockroaches and stinkbugs. She says it loudly—my grandma isn't afraid of anyone, not even Death. She says Death is her best friend and she doesn't mind going away.

Mama gets upset when she says that and starts to cry. Varsha, who likes big words, says it's all RELATIVE and our town is no better no worse than anyone else's town. And she doesn't really care because a town is a town is a town and she isn't planning on leaving. Varsha likes me to agree with everything she says because we'll always be together, and if I don't she'll call on the Ghosts to teach me a lesson.

The night before my baby brother died I was kneeling on my bed. I was looking out at the dark from the window. I blew on the cold black glass to make a fog circle and wrote my name on it. But I wiped it off quickly with the hem of my pyjama top, just in case, because you never know who's watching. There are creatures out there who can steal my name and after that nobody would know who I was not even my own Mama, Varsha said.

I knew she wasn't asleep. She was lying in her bed beside mine, her eyes shut tight, her hands pressed against her ears, singing so we couldn't hear the sounds coming from Mama and Papa's bedroom down the corridor. Or maybe she was sending up one of her long prayers to Jesus Krishna Buddha and Martin Luther King. My sister taught me the names of all these gods and ghosts—she discovered them inside books in Papa's book-room. She said they were good ghosts and would always help us in our time of need.

All of a sudden we heard a small sound. I thought it was a puppy. Like the sound a puppy makes when someone kicks it. So Varsha jumped out of bed and ran to open our door. I saw Mama fall out of her room just like that, like she was leaning against the door and it suddenly opened so she fell out. One minute she was inside with Papa and the next moment she thumped out, with a hard sound. Papa's feet looked like a giant's. We ran to Mama. I tried to lift her up.

"Are you okay, Mama?" I think Varsha was really scared too.

"Yes, yes, I am." Mama sounded like she was coughing and she pushed our hands away. "What are you both doing here? Go back to your room, go, go . . .". She shoved us hard, making me nearly fall so I wanted to cry too.

I could see inside Mama's bedroom which has wallpaper of yellow and pink roses and a giant bed made of black wood. There are thick gold curtains for hiding behind when I am angry with Varsha or Papa is angry with me. There is a huge dresser where Mama sits in the morning after she has had a bath. She looks like a queen when she is combing out her long hair. Papa's huge shadow climbed up the wall, his head became a big dark splash on the ceiling. He was shouting something but I don't know what.

He came out of the bedroom and his shadow climbed down and followed him. He glared at Mama lying in a pile. "Eh? I said why don't you ever listen to me? Eh?"

He kicked at her foot and Mama said, "Don't, don't, please don't! The children are here." She put one hand on her stomach and she used the other hand to push herself up and she got up and walked slowly back into the bedroom. "Vikram, think of the baby, he will be hurt, please don't—"

Then Varsha pulled me away and Papa shut the door in our faces so we stood there which made me feel very bad because Varsha was yanking yanking at her hair the way she does when she's upset and we had to listen to sounds on the other side of the door, like Mama and Papa kept bumping into furniture. Varsha and me, we heard Mama start crying and then everything went creepy quiet.

"Should we pray to Jesus and Martin Luther King?" I asked Varsha. Sometimes the gods and ghosts we prayed to were asleep or out helping other kids who were in trouble and couldn't come to us. Varsha was holding my hand really hard but that was a good hand holding. Varsha said, "No, let's go down see Akka. She'll make it all okay." So we went down the stairs to our grandmother who was almost a ghost herself but she was very good at making us feel safe and making it better.

Akka was sleeping. She was wrapped tight in blankets like a mummy. Varsha leaned over and poked her cheek which was like a hole under her cheekbone and whispered, "Akka, wake up Akka."

"What? What happened? Is it you, God? Have you come for me at last?" Akka mumbled. Then she woke up suddenly and stared at us with her eyes white and big, which I could see because of the light of the night-lamp. Her hair was all wild and blowey around her face.

"No Akka, it's us, me and Hem, we're scared. There were noises upstairs." Varsha climbed into Akka's bed. I crawled under the blankets which were always there even in the middle of summer. I like the dried-up old smells of Vicks Vaporub and coconut oil that Mama massages on Akka's chest and back, and medicines which she has to take for her heart and her blood pressure and to keep the sugar in her body low. I asked why she had to do that and Akka explained it was because she was getting too sweet and the ants would come and eat her up if she didn't reduce her sweetness. I licked Akka's hand but she didn't taste of anything other than dry skin but I like that anyway.

"Was this noise from your Papa's room, my children?" Akka asked.

"Yes Akka," Varsha said.

"Yes Akka," I said too, because my sister knows everything in the world.

"Was your mother okay, my children?" Akka asked, putting her arm around the two of us even though she could barely reach that far.

"I don't know for sure." Varsha's voice was shaky like she was still trying not to cry.

"It's okay, it's okay," Akka said. Her voice was shivery too.

That was when Varsha started to cry. Akka pulled us really close, as close as she could. "That's all right my darling, don't feel so bad. It's only a dream, tomorrow it will be fine." Then she pushed my sister away suddenly and held her nose and whispered, "Who did it? Which of you did it? Let loose a big one, a gas bomb, enh? Come on now, tell your Akka!"

"Oh Akka, that's not funny," Varsha groaned.

I giggled. "Not me Akka, not me, it must have been her"—holding my nose too to show I was not the one.

"Unh-unh, wasn't me," Varsha said. I could hear a smiling in her voice now. She tickled Akka and said, "It must be you Akka, nobody else here in this room."

Akka cackled. "The loud fart makes the most noise, the medium one is neither here nor there, the quiet one it is that makes your life a stinking misery." She tickled Varsha back and whispered, "Tell, tell the truth, who let it out? Not me, not me for sure. Aha! I know who it is, this little boy with a big stinky stomach." It was an old joke that Akka said to make us laugh when we were sad. She's told us a zillion times but I still like it. She waved the air with one hand and went *hee-hee-hee* like in the cartoons. She doesn't have many teeth, Akka, and her wide open mouth is gummy pink, and her gold bangles, two for my wife and two for Varsha when we grow up and get married, go *chink-a-chink*. Sometimes she got Mama to dress her up in the morning like she was going to a party, big shiny earrings, flowers in her white hair, and black stuff around her eyes to make them look big as a deer's. She said it was fun and made us dress up too sometimes.

There are lots of comforters on Akka's bed because she's always cold. She says her bones are filled with ice from having lived for so many years in Canada. What would happen if Akka turned too warm and the ice inside her melted? Or if her bones cracked from the pressure of the ice *crick-crack* like the hearts of trees in winter time? When I tell my secrets to Tree and then I put my ear against it, sometimes I can hear its heart bursting apart from the water inside turning into ice then melting and freezing again. I thought maybe the water would flow out of Akka like many rivers, wetting Varsha and me as we hugged her tight, soaking our nice warm bed, messing up the floor. Then our Papa would come thundering down, his eyes red, his hands raised to smack us. He would never touch Akka of course. She was his mama. But I was scared because he would blame Varsha and me for the water from our grandmother's bones that dripped down and made a mighty flood.

"He can't help it because he has a demon in his blood, in his marrow," Akka whispered. I could feel her old breath like a feather on my face. "Your father, from his own father he got it. It breaks my heart, it does it does."

"Is it the demon that lives on that side of the gate, Akka, the one Mama told us about?" I asked. We were never to wander out beyond the gate especially after dark because a demon lived there who ate children for breakfastlunchdinnertea.

"No, this one is embroidered into the pattern of his skin, it is coiled in his intestines," Akka said. "A demon laid a curse on Papa's father's head when he was a boy, just like the wicked fairy in Sleeping Beauty." She scowled ferociously. She is always angry when she talks about my dead grandpa. Varsha says it's because he was mean to her. "Then the same demon laid an evil eye on your Papa because he was so good and handsome."

So I see a large mean eye floating in the air above Papa's head, shooting out wicked lightning bolts at him, turning him from a good child and making him an angry roaring demon man. What if the eye decides to look at me? Or Varsha? Maybe we will turn into a monster like our Papa. Then there will be nobody left to take care of Mama and me. Akka is way too old and pretty soon she'll be dead, she keeps telling us so. "I shouldn't be alive!" She wheezes and laughs in her voice that cracks, and she looks up at the ceiling as if god is sitting up there on the chocolate brown fan with the big fat light hanging from it. "Why is that fellow up there keeping me here? Hey you, do you hear, send me a ladder, it's time for me to climb up or down, I don't know and don't care. All I want is that ladder. Too long too long I have been here. I am bored I am tired I am old. Hey you, listen to me!"

But another time Akka said Papa was the way he was not because of a demon inside him but because of the genes that came to him from his father Mr. J.K. Dharma. Genes are something you get from ancestors, like our house and money, and cut glass decanters and the green sofa that has a leg missing and has to be propped up with a brick made of newspaper, and Mama's jewellery which

Varsha says is hers because she is a girl and girls get their mother's stuff. I don't think that's fair since Mama is only her stepmother and she already has Real Mother's jewels. But when I say so, Varsha gets mad at me. She says she will curse me with the evil eye if I ever ever *ever* again say that Mama is not hers. She will curse me and she will summon all the ghosts in the world to carry me away and torture me. "She is mine, you are mine, everybody in this house is mine, you miserable runt." She screamed this at me. She scared me so much I decided to stay under my bed for a whole entire morning.

"Your Papa was a good boy," Akka said bitterly. I watched the little drops of water that leaked slowly out of the corners of her eyes. They caught in the pouchy skin underneath, and then spilled down her cheeks. Varsha wiped them away gently, licking her fingers like she was licking away our grandmother's sadness. "But he got his father's genes, he got his father's demons. That's why he gets so angry, my children. That's why."

I don't like thinking about demons torturing my Papa's intestines, making him go crazy when he looks at us or at Mama. When he opens his mouth to yawn or laugh I wait for the demon to come out from inside of him in a puff of dark smoke. I'm sure I can see it moving around.

"Can't a doctor cure our Papa?" I asked.

Akka said some illnesses have no cure except death. "When I see what he does to your mother, it hurts my heart."

And I hugged Akka back because my heart was hurting too.

When we woke up, everything was okay again. Mama was in the kitchen. She was making scrambled eggs for us. Papa was sitting at the table all dressed and ready to go to work.

"Did you sleep well, my pieces of the moon?" Mama asked when we came into the kitchen. She smiled at me. She had a bruise on her face just below her eye. It was like a purple-pink flower.

Varsha said, "Yes Mama we did, thank you."

I looked at my sister because she'd forgotten about the night time. "Mama, you got hurt." I pointed to her face. "Papa, look!"

"Did I? Where?" She smiled at us all this time.

"On your face," I said. "It's a funny colour."

"Really?" She shrugged. "I must have bumped into something last night."

"Too much of an imagination, just like your mother." Papa slapped Mama's bottom and pulled her close to him. She touched Papa's hair but her eyes looked at Varsha and me. Her eyes were trying to say something to us without words but I wasn't sure what it was.

Then Papa left for work. When we were all dressed Mama walked Varsha and me to the bus stop at the end of the road, all of us wrapped tight, holding hands because the snow was blowing so hard. If we held hands we would be fine even if we couldn't see anything and got lost.

Varsha said if we did get lost it would be together as a family and a family that sticks together succeeds together.

"Remember, don't tell anyone at school anything, understand?" Mama's voice was coming out of her muffler like it was all wrapped up in wool.

Varsha was kicking at the snow as she walked. She picked up a fallen branch and hit the air hard with it. *Flick-flickety-flick!* It sounded like Papa's belt just before it lands on my skin when I've done something bad andletdowntheDharmaname, and I thought, Don't tell anyone what.

Anu's Notebook

August 22. The children are just hanging around again today. They must be bored. No other kids to play with here—they don't bring friends home. I think they've been snooping inside my hut; some of my things aren't where I remember putting them. A few days ago, I returned from a trip to town to find my notebook open. I'm certain I'd closed it when I left the house. I must lock the door, which I don't always remember to do—the emptiness of this place makes me feel I'm safe. Perhaps I'm being too suspicious, but they are an odd pair those two. I see them often roaming around the property. Their favourite spot seems to be a spectacularly tall old conifer some way off to the right of my house.

Yesterday afternoon I wandered up to them, curious about what they were up to. They had their faces pressed against the trunk of the tree, arms wrapped around it as far as they could reach. I think they were singing, or maybe chanting something in low tones. The girl noticed me first. She leapt away from the tree and really glowered at me.

"What are you doing here?" she demanded. "You can't come here."

"Why not?" I tried to sound mild, not offended as I was. "Nobody told me I was forbidden to go anywhere on this property."

"Well, I'm telling you now, so make sure you don't come here again," she said peremptorily.

"Why? Is there something special about this spot?" I was not appreciating her ordering me around.

"Yes, it's *our* place. This is *our* tree. You can't come here. You can't touch *our* tree."

"*Our* tree," Hemant repeated.

The little boy is, as usual, glued to his sister. If I spot one, I know the other is not too far away. He never says anything without his sister's permission, and when he does, it's to repeat a bit of whatever she has just said, like a weird echo. They don't like me, they made that quite clear the first day when I arrived, when they crashed into the room, scowling and furious. Even my bribes of pastries and other goodies that I take over to the house haven't made much of a dent in their hostility. They gobble it up, thank me because they're supposed to, and disappear off somewhere. They seem to blame me because their mother hadn't gone to meet them the day I arrived, the pampered brats!

"We waited for you!" Varsha had said, glaring at her stepmother.

"I am sorry, Vashi." Suman tried to hug the girl, who evaded her arms and continued to sulk. "I am sorry, it won't happen again."

"We waited and waited and Hem was getting really terrified something had happened to you." Varsha sounded like a schoolteacher and Suman an errant child, and I wondered how on earth Suman allowed the little bully to push her around like that. Now I understand the family dynamic a little better, I realize Suman lets *everyone* push her around.

"You're old enough to bring your little brother home, aren't you?" I said in the kind of voice I use with my brother's kids. I shouldn't have poked my nose in since I was a stranger just arrived, but I guess I thought I was being friendly and aunty-ish. The girl obviously didn't.

"Who are *you*?" she said, giving me a look that's become familiar to me—a mixture of scorn and irritation.

"She is our new tenant, Varsha," Suman said. "Anu Krishnan. I told you she was arriving today, don't you remember?"

The boy had climbed onto his grandmother's bed. "MY grandmother," he said in a baby voice, kissing Akka's face extravagantly.

I smiled at him and said, "Lucky boy to have such a wonderful grandma!" or some such, I don't remember. I do recall with embarrassment that the girl irritated me so much I was ready to smack her. I reminded myself, as

I find myself doing practically every time I talk to her, that I am an adult and childish spite is not an adult option. The boy continued to stare suspiciously at me with those prominent eyes of his, as if he expected to catch me red-handed at something. But Akka seems genuinely attached to the boy and his awful sister. She stroked their heads and fussed over them and seemed not to notice they were ill-mannered brats. I was definitely not a part of the cuddly unit of three that afternoon—and when Suman started clucking about school and homework I decided it was time for me to leave.

The girl is a malevolent little spider with her bony face and arching, well-marked eyebrows above giant eyes. She wouldn't be bad-looking except when she smiles—she reveals a set of sharp, irregular teeth which resemble the coconut scraper my grandmother used to bring along with her from India when she came to visit us. I wonder why her parents haven't bothered to get them fixed. Once her teeth are straightened out, she might end up looking like her gorgeous mother Helen. Suman told me she's thirteen, but she appears much younger because she's so small.

The boy is not pretty at all, which is surprising since his father is still, I admit, very handsome and his mother amiable-looking if rather downtrodden. There's a sense of nervous frailty about him. He scuttles along on a pair of Pinocchio legs. Suman said he's sickly, nearly died when he was a baby, so the females in the family treat him as if he is a piece of antique china. Horribly spoilt, in other words. He appears quite healthy to me. Ugly as a troll, but healthy as one too. And will prove to be as long-lived since trolls live for thousands of years.

Suman puzzles me. She's clearly a thoughtful woman and—now she's no longer so nervously shy—she's kind with me (and generous too). But she behaves like a doormat around her family. These pretences we've had to concoct about my being in the house because of Akka, and the secretive food business!

Vikram's mother Akka is the best of the lot. She must have been quite something when she was young. I like her, she reminds me of my own grandmother with her shrewd eyes and her acerbic wit. She is well read, speaks several Indian languages in addition to the Queen's English. I can't imagine what she's doing in a dump like this, or how she arrived here in the first place, but I suspect I'll hear all about it soon enough. She's chatty and fun to be with, and tells me all sorts of stories with great gusto when she's feeling well, though she's more or less confined to her bed. Apparently a stroke some years ago weakened her considerably, then a few months later a fall broke something in her back and now she's always in a great deal of pain. Suman tells me that it's sometimes so bad Akka can't even lie down, and then she has to spend entire days sitting in an odd wooden structure that is a bizarre cross between an armchair and one of those old-fashioned raised wooden potties. I've seen her tethered to that chair, and I mean that literally, with bedsheets torn into long strips that wind around her body and the back of the wooden contraption, so she won't topple out in her sleep. It seems barbaric to keep the old woman tied to a chair. Surely there's something else that can be done, something properly medical? I asked Suman why they didn't consult a doctor.

She was vague and guarded. "We did. And then Vikram's friend, Gopal, who knows about these things, said this is the best way."

The best way? To keep an old woman bound to her chair, sitting for days on end? I'm not sure what to do—I feel I have to speak to Suman and Vikram about it again. I of all people understand how terrifying it is for an immigrant family to release their elderly parent into care in a strange home with food and customs frighteningly foreign to her at that age. But she needs better care. It's all wrong. This Gopal sounds like a quack to me, and I said as much.

Suman gave me a blank look. "I don't know, you must ask Vikram about it. He took Akka to the hospital and they said there wasn't anything they could do for her at her age without causing other problems. Forty-sixty percent chance she might be healed—or become a vegetable, they said. So Vikram says this is the best decision. Vikram knows."

I hear these phrases at every turn—*Vikram knows, Papa knows, Papa says, Vikram says.* He seems to be god around these parts, my classmate Vikram. I'm beginning to think that everybody in the house is terrified of him. If I want to be spiteful and childish—as I confess I'm tempted to be when those brats are around—all I need to do to get them to behave is threaten to complain to their father. All the bluster leaves them and they turn into a pair of frightened little kids. Which makes me feel like shit.

Hemant

My baby brother would've been five years younger than me if he'd got born. He was very tiny. He died because he was a PREEMIE. Varsha told me. Mama was going to call him Vasanth which means Spring. I would have liked to be an older brother. *My* brother. *Ours*, Varsha said.

After school one day Mama showed us X-ray photos of our brother. He was like a ghost floating in white stuff, sucking his thumb. The stuff is called an AMNIOTIC SAC and contains water. It protects the baby. I was the one who spotted the baby's ear shaped like a shell and I asked if he could hear things from this side. Could he hear the yelling? Or the songs Mama sang to him? Could he hear me? Or Varsha? Could he hear the woman who Mama says sings in the moon when it's round and full? "Yes, he can," Mama said. "He can hear every single thing, so be careful what you say, Hem. Your little brother is listening to you and learning from you." She was sure the baby was a boy. She said she could *feel* it in her heart.

I believe mostly everything my mother tells me. I will be an astronaut. Varsha will own a circus. Butterflies are spirits of good people. Moths are the souls of the wicked. Papa will always love me and Varsha. The way he does when he's in a good mood. When he drives us for ice creams and makes us giggle. When he says he's sorry.

But I don't believe Mama when she said she fell down the stairs and broke her arm. Or bumped into the furniture in the dark, or that she gave herself a black eye when she was pulling out a STUBBORN root in the garden. Even though Varsha twists my arm hard and says I'm a naughty little liar and Papa and Mama are the happiest people in the world and we're the happiest family in the world. If I have any lies to tell, Varsha says, I have to whisper them to Tree and nobody else or one of the six hundred and seventy-three ghosts who live between our house and the sky will come and drag me away by the ears into the black lake and I will be trapped like the fish that float under the ice in winter.

Varsha said especially I was not to lie when we had to call 911, and the ambulance people came to take Mama away to the hospital because the baby was slipping out of her tummy too soon. She said if the ambulance people asked I was to tell them Mama fell down the stairs by accident. So I told them. When Mama came back home without my brother I went to Tree and told it everything. I told how Mama had fallen out of her room when Papa was being a wicked giant. I told how I wasn't lying even though Varsha said I was. Tree listened quietly and then it said *shhh, shhh, shhh* and then it was okay for a while. So I was not so scared.

After my baby brother died Mama wept for six days and seven nights. I counted. Then she went quiet. Then she began to search, search, search. I was at home sick. I saw her. Varsha told me she was looking for her passport, so she could leave us in Merrit's Point and go away to India. That scared me. What would we do without our Mama? But Varsha said she couldn't leave because she'd hidden the passport. She showed me where she hid it behind Grandpa's photograph.

"But if you tell her, she will go away without us. And I will be very angry and call a slimy ghost to eat your brains."

Mama was turning things upside down. She checked under my mattress. She looked inside all my drawers and inside my cupboard. When we had lunch she checked inside the rice tin and the sugar tin. So I asked, "What are you searching for Mama?" even though I knew but I pretended.

She pressed a finger to her lips. "I am looking for my happiness, Hemu. Can you help me find it?" But then she gave a huge sigh. "My passport, Hem, have you seen it anywhere?"

So I said, "What's a passport Mama?" even though I knew.

"A magic book that will let us go all the way to India," Mama said. Then she placed a finger against her mouth again. "But this is our secret, okay Hem?

Don't tell anybody. Not Papa. Or your sister. Promise?"

"Yes Mama, I promise."

"On my head Hem, promise on my *head*." Mama knelt down and put my hand on her head. "Now if you tell anyone, I will die. You don't want that, do you bayboo?"

I promised and I promised. Mama's secret felt very heavy inside me. "But what if I *have* to tell somebody? What if the secret just wants to come out? Then what do I do? Sometimes my face hurts from not telling."

Mama looked around and around the room, like we were being followed by monsters. Then she smiled at me and hugged me hard. "Do as Akka told you—tell it to the trees. They know how to keep secrets."

So I told Tree how Mama was looking for her passport. I told it that she wanted to run far away to India. But Varsha saw me.

"I hope you've told me what you're telling Tree, Hem." She crossed her arms and her eyebrows met across her forehead. I knew she was mad at me. She owns me because she saw me first in the whole wide world and I'm not to keep secrets from her. "You know what will happen if you haven't, don't you?"

I nodded. She would call the demons from the other side of our gate and they would carry me away. So I told her Mama was looking for her passport and she wanted to go all the way back to India so she could be happy like she was when she was a girl.

"Silly Mama," Varsha said. "How can she think of doing such a shameful thing? It will bring our name down to dust, and what will happen to us if she leaves? Good thing you told me, Hem. Now we will have to watch Mama extra carefully, won't we?"

"Are you going to tell Papa?"

Varsha thought about that for two seconds and then she shook her head. "No, not right now."

"What if she finds her passport when we're in school and runs away without us?"

"She will never find her passport. I know for sure." Varsha gave me a mysterious sort of smile.

After some time Mama stopped searching for her passport. My baby brother's ghost went away. Varsha said. Everything was okay, Varsha wasn't mad at me for a long time, Papa was nice to Mama, and I stopped feeling scared.

Then one morning Anu came to be our back-house tenant.

I think she's pretty. Varsha doesn't like her. Beauty is as Beauty does. Varsha says. But I like Anu. Not as much as I love Mama. I love Mama so much I can't breathe sometimes. Not as much as I love Varsha and Akka. I like Anu more than Papa. Which makes me feel like I'm a wicked boy. Varsha says I am *not* to like Anu. She is an INTERLOPER my sister says. She's an evil spirit who has come to our house to steal our Mama and it's our duty to make sure she doesn't.

I whisper my secrets to Tree and feel better.

So all of us will be safe for ever and ever.

But still.

Should I tell Mama?

Anu's Notebook

September 15. Glad to report the kids are back at school and my lunch service has resumed. I am growing chubby but have no regrets at all. There are some days when Suman doesn't show up at my cottage. When she does, she never talks about what has kept her away, and even though I am tempted to ask, I feel uncertain about prying. I know for sure now that there is something not quite right about the state of affairs in the Dharma household. But I am not clear what it is.

October 3. The light is low and golden and the shadows long. The leaves have turned and it's nippy. There is an air of regret hanging over everything. I find myself heaving great big sighs all the time. I think I need a break from this writing solitude to reconnect with my own life for a bit. Perhaps over the Christmas break a visit with my brothers and my nephews— nice, uncomplicated kids would be a pleasant change. I need to see Mummy, too—not that she has any idea

who *I* am. It hurts me to see her like that—so frail
and lost.

October 16. Today, along with my daily lunch, Suman
brought a request from Akka. She wanted to see me at
three-thirty, for tea and snacks. "If it is not too much
trouble," she added.

I was glad of an excuse to get away from my own
company and I am curious about the old woman, so naturally I went. As soon as I showed up, Akka said, apropos
of nothing, "Do you know I can speak six languages?"

By now I am used to these odd openings to conversations that depend on Akka's moods or on the
memories she wants to mine that afternoon. If I am
patient and ask the right questions, we might meander
into interesting territory. Sometimes, though, she is not
entirely there, and doesn't make much sense, referring
erratically to events, people, places I do not know, a
hodgepodge of information all wrapped up in stories
and songs which she delivers in various languages. So
this afternoon, I was relieved to see, she was full of
beans and completely lucid.

"That's amazing!" I exclaimed, genuinely impressed.

Akka snorted. "What is amazing is that I used none
of my talents. My knowledge has rotted from disuse.
What use all that knowledge, tell me? I ended up in this
Jehannum where nobody cares about my past or my
abilities." She brooded in silence for a few seconds
while Suman poured out the tea. She never contributes

anything to these conversations. I wonder what the two women speak about when I'm not there. They are obviously close.

"I should have been like you," Akka started off again. "Free bird, comes and goes as she pleases, does what she wants, eh, Suman? Wouldn't you like Anu's life?"

Suman held her mug of tea tight between her two small hands.

"Come, come, Sumana, you can say what you want here in this room. Nothing will happen to you, you know that!" Akka urged, looking kindly at her daughter-in-law.

Suman gave me a quick glance, full of subtleties I cannot understand, but said nothing. The conversation threatened to wind down.

"I'll bet your son is proud of you, Akka." I tried to start things up again. "And your husband too, when he was alive. No?"

Akka turned her head to look out of the window. It is unlike her to have no ready, sharp retort. Finally she turned back to me. "We hated each other, my husband and I. His opinion mattered nothing to me, he was a drunkard and he deserved to die." She clasped her wrinkled hands on her chest and shut her eyes. She was sitting on that chair of hers, which is padded with pillows, bolsters, sheets and so many other things that it looks like a bag lady's stash.

I stared at her, surprised at the venom in her voice. "I'm sure you don't really mean that, do you, Akka? Nobody deserves to die, do they?"

"*He* did. And good riddance to bad rubbish is what I say."

Silence again. This time I didn't try to bridge it with any comment. This house is so full of odd currents. I am no angel and my brother and I don't always see eye to eye over many things, and my husband thought I was a fucking bitch, as he was fond of calling me in the last year of our marriage. But this family takes the prize for dysfunctional.

Akka called Suman over to adjust her pillows and once she was comfortable again turned and smiled at me. "He was a bastard," she said pleasantly this time. "He had bad genes. My karma and poor Suman's that he passed these on to my son. I am delighted he is no longer with us." She dusted her hands together emphatically. Then she looked at the clock and said, "Ayyo! Suman, go and fetch the children, otherwise we'll have another drama here.

"This America is getting too big for its boots," she said after Suman left. She loves politics, enjoys arguing with me about current events. "One of these days they will learn their lesson!"

"Who will teach it to them? They're too powerful." I am always mildly defensive about the U.S. I like that country, the energy with which it approaches everything. I think their cultural life, the arts, literature, dance, music, is youthful and dynamic. I had loved living in New York, and the cutthroat atmosphere on Wall Street suited my own ambitious nature at first. I thrived on competition.

"Haven't you heard the story of the ant and the elephant?" Akka smiled slyly at me. "Let me tell you."

I settled down, feeling like a small child waiting for her granny to tell bedtime stories—a lovely feeling.

"Once, a long time ago, when the sky was green and the ground was blue, an arrogant rogue of an elephant went about wreaking havoc in the jungle. He started to tear down the branches of a tree on which a sparrow had built her nest.

"'Please, sir, your highness, your majesty,' she pleaded as the elephant shook and ripped the tree with his mighty trunk. 'My babies are in the nest, please leave this tree alone or they will fall and die. Wait until they have learned to fly and then do what you will with my house.'

"The elephant laughed and continued to destroy the tree until the nest collapsed, killing the baby sparrows.

"An ant heard the poor little bird wailing at the loss of her family, and when he found out what the wicked elephant had done, he told the bird, 'This is untenable, dear Mrs. Sparrow. We'll have to find a way to teach this arrogant elephant a lesson.'

"'But he is so big and we are so tiny,' the bird said. 'What can we possibly do to him?'

"'Don't worry, I'll think of a plan,' the ant promised.

"The next day, he waited until the elephant was asleep and crept into his anus, biting him hard. The elephant ran here and there trying to get the ant out but could not. The sparrow flew about his head chirping and irritating the elephant, driving him towards the edge of a cliff. Mad with pain and confused by the bird in his face, the elephant did not see where he was going and dropped over the cliff to his death.

"The moral of the story," Akka said, shaking a transparent finger at me, "is that the mighty do not always win. You don't have to be as big as an elephant to get your revenge!"

I was still recovering from the savagery of the story when she added, "Like I did."

I stared at her. "Like you did what?"

"Got my revenge," the old woman said.

The door banged open just then, the children rushed into the room, and that strange unexplained remark was lost in the general chaos.

Akka held out her arms to Hemant from her chair. "Come to me, my little darling. Tell me all about your day." The boy kissed his grandmother, then disengaged himself and climbed onto her bed as he usually does, shoes and all, and sat there like a prince while his mother removed them for him.

"What were you talking about with *her*?" Varsha demanded.

"I was telling Anu our favourite story," Akka said. "About the elephant and the bird and the ant."

This is their favourite story? Why am I not surprised? And why did Akka tell it to me? And what did she mean by her comment about revenge?

"But it's *our* story." Varsha sounded just like her little brother.

"A story needs as many listeners as it can get, Vashi," Akka said. "Otherwise it might sicken and die."

Varsha stomped out of the room and Akka sighed. "That girl needs friends. She is too much at home. At her age—"

"*I* am her friend," Hemant piped up.

"Yes, darling, you are." Akka smiled at him.

Hemant gave me a petulant look which made me want to smack him. "When is she leaving? I'm hungry."

I stood, determined not to leave until I wanted to do so—the kid isn't going to push me around, that's for sure—and walked over to a collection of faded photographs in small ornate frames on a round table near the window, picking one up at random. It was the same as the large one in Vikram's office, of a tidy-looking man with a moustache and a distant look in his eyes, like he has removed himself from the scenery a long time ago. His thick dark hair is neatly parted on the left side of his head. He wears a suit a couple of sizes too large for his small frame, as if it had been borrowed from somebody bigger. He has small, deep-set eyes and a determined mouth. Perched above that mouth, like a furry caterpillar, is a moustache that does nothing other than emphasize his long nose and plump mouth. So this was Mr. J.K. Dharma, the conveyer of bad genes, the builder of this palace in the back of beyond, the progenitor of the family Dharma, and Akka's despised spouse. Why, then, I wondered, does she keep a photograph of him?

"To remind me that he is dead and I am not," the old lady said, as if she'd read my thoughts—and perhaps she had, the old witch.

"Did he die a long time ago?" I asked.

"Did who die?" the brat asked, looking from me to Akka and back with those long-lashed eyes, much like Suman's, and which seem too big for his thin face.

"Your grandfather," I replied, with a friendly expression on my face for Akka's benefit. "Can you go and ask your Mama if she can make me a cup of tea?"

"Ask her yourself," Hemant said. "You're not the boss of me!"

Fortunately, Akka decided to take my side. "Hemu, that's not a nice thing to say to Anu Aunty," she reprimanded, elevating me from tenant to aunt, in typical Indian style. "Go, tell Suman to make us all some tea, I would also like a hot drink."

"She's not my aunt," muttered Hemant, but he left the room without further argument.

"So, when did he die, then?" I asked again.

"Oh, when Vikram was in high school. Years ago."

"That's terrible. You must have been so young yourself!"

Akka started to say something when Suman entered like a djinn with tea and another plate of pakoras. "You're amazing. We just sent Hemant to ask for tea and voilà, here it is!" I said admiringly. I'm getting used to being waited on!

Suman smiled shyly, set the tray down on a side table

and fussed with the tea things. The sun drifted in through the open window and lit up her face, giving her a soft, delicate prettiness.

"What were you talking about? Both of you look like conspirators!" She handed a cup of hot tea to me.

"She was asking me about my drunken lout of a husband," Akka said. She raised her cup to her mouth, holding it tight with both hands, the knuckle bones threatening to break through the thin, taut skin. "I was telling her how glad I was when he died." She caught sight of Suman's appalled face and snapped, "What? Henh? Why are you looking at me like that?"

"It's not nice to tell visitors such things, Akka."

"Tchah! It happened a long time ago. What matter if I tell the truth now?" Akka cackled with delight—whether it was at the imperviousness of old age or the pleasure of having an audience, it was hard to tell. "You want to know how he died? Henh? He froze to death. Right outside our front door. And me fast asleep inside. Didn't hear the doorbell, didn't hear him knocking away, bang, bang, bang! They found him the next morning, propped up against the front door. Frozen solid, like a statue. God punished him for making my life a misery!"

There was a small sound behind me. I turned to see Varsha coming in, her face scrubbed and innocent, her arms full of school books.

"You have to go now. I have homework to do," she said with a pointed look at me. "Akka, I need your help."

"Oh no, let her finish her tea at least, Vashi," Suman said. "And she hasn't even tasted the pakoras."

"I can't concentrate on my homework if she stays," Varsha said.

"Yes and the child's school work comes first," Akka added, shutting her eyes.

"Take the pakoras with you." Suman urged.

Obviously I was dismissed. But I left reluctantly, certain there was more to Akka's story and sorry not to have got it out of the old lady. Had she really been asleep while Mr. J.K. Dharma froze to death outside the front door? He must have rung the bell and knocked. Was it possible that she had *allowed* him to die in the cold?

November 10. I met the famous Chanchal and Gopal-the-quack Aggarwal at the grocery store this morning. I was about to line up to pay my bill when a woman tapped my shoulder. She knew who I was, of course.

"Hello, hello, it is me, Chanchal," she said when I turned around, startled. She is a tall, bony woman in her late fifties with a striking face and abundant white hair which she was wearing pulled back in a bun. Her husband Gopal is about the same height, with absolutely no hair on his head, as if to compensate for his wife's thick tresses. Chanchal does all the talking, with Gopal putting in a few words here and there with an air of great certainty.

"You know me? I am the friend of Akka and Vikram." Her smile pushed up her already high cheekbones even farther. I wonder if she has some Pahadi blood in her veins—those high cheekbones, the golden skin, the almond-shaped eyes. Even though her last name suggests someone from Uttar Pradesh, her features indicate other influences.

"Of course, how nice to meet you at last! And you must be Gopal. I've heard about you from Suman."

"Good things only, I am hoping!" Chanchal laughed, and Gopal nodded in a friendly way. I turned away to pay at the till, and then I waited politely for the Aggarwals to finish with their own purchases. I reminded myself that I have all the time in the world to wait for people, chat, discover things about this community. It is a luxury I've granted myself and I shall make full use of it.

"You must come home for tea," Chanchal said as they gathered up their parcels.

"Most certainly. When would be a good day for you?"

"Now, come now. I made some fresh naan khatai, you know our naan khatai?"

"Very good taste." Gopal added his bit and fell silent.

"Are you sure you want me to land up right now, this minute?" I knew they meant it. The generous hospitality reminded me of my own parents, who often brought home strangers for chai or lunch, who occasionally turned into lifelong friends. "Mr. Aggarwal? I don't want to interrupt your work."

"Fully retired. No work. Memsahib is telling you to come, you must come." I discovered later that he never refers to his wife by name, only ironically as Memsahib.

"Yes, yes, why would I ask otherwise, tell me! You will come with us now. Gopal, you drive our car home and I will follow with Anu in hers."

Chanchal chattered away on the short drive to her home, telling me she has two children—a son and a daughter. "Both married, both gone to U.S. They are always begging us to come and live with them. But my husband is telling me, it is better to have independence as long as we can manage. Children are loving, but things change when they get married. That is how it is. I want to go back to India, but Gopal is not liking the idea. He is totally foreigner, you know. India is very far away for him. But for me, it is still here." She thumped her chest vigorously. "And here." Touched her forehead. "I feel sad all the time when I am thinking of India. Especially now when winter is coming."

"Everyone tells me about winter here. I'm originally from Vancouver, and I've seen some bad winters in New York, so I'm not a wallflower, but I'm getting positively nervous," I said.

"It gives me palpitations of the heart," Chanchal said solemnly. "That is why I go to India in December. Gopal says that the cold is not good for the heart. He could have been a doctor, he is very good with such matters. Natural talent."

"Really?" I hoped my tone was not too cynical.

"Yes, it runs in his family. Natural doctors all of them—his grandmother and mother and father also. Without him I would be dead by now, you know."

"You are not well? You look good to me." I looked at her with some surprise.

"Appearance is deceiving. I am very sick inside. Headache. Stomach problems. Legs not working sometimes. Heart. Blood pressure. Cholesterol very high. Poor Gopal has to look after me all the time, you know."

After giving me a long list of ailments that afflicted her, Chanchal moved on to the brilliance of her children and their educational qualifications, their jobs, their salaries, their cars and how many they possessed, the size of their homes, and so on. The Aggarwals live in a large house not too far from town, shaded by a great old sugar maple in full red, autumnal glory. Their garden is in a much better state of repair than the Dharma's, even though it is the end of the growing season, when everything goes to seed and looks ragged. The plants have all been cut down, shrubs tied with string, leaves raked off the lawn, and the beds heavily mulched in preparation for winter. All apparently Gopal's doing. He may have bizarre ideas as a self-made doctor, but he seems to love his garden.

"Keeps him busy, otherwise these retired men are problem," Chanchal informed me when I remarked on how neat everything looked.

"Gopal, we are going in. You will bring the groceries," she commanded as we passed the silent Gopal, who had got in just ahead of us.

"Yes, Memsahib," he murmured. His small eyes met mine and he smiled slightly. "Her wish is my command."

"Talk, talk, talk," complained Chanchal, dragging me up the path to the front door. "He never does anything unless he wants to. All show for your benefit."

Like the Dharmas', her house was spotlessly clean and very neat.

"Sit, sit, be comfortable, I will make some hot tea for us."

While I waited, I looked around at the walls. There were several framed family photographs, a large print of a kitten with a pink ribbon round its neck, and at least a dozen garish prints of the god Krishna. Gopal entered with the groceries and I got up to help him.

"Oh, no, no, Memsahib will scold me for making our guest work. Please sit." He smiled his ironic little smile again.

I sat back in my cushiony armchair and a few minutes later Chanchal strode in like an ungainly goddess bearing a tray loaded with tea things and several bowls of snacks.

"Your children are good-looking," I said. "Take after you."

"Thank you, so kind you are." She looked pleased. "You are also very pretty. Gopal, isn't she pretty? Looks like your sister's daughter, no?"

"Yes, yes," Gopal agreed with his wife. It was becoming apparent that he never disagrees with her.

"He likes you," Chanchal informed me. "If you have any health problems, you ask him for advice. He is very good."

"Yes, yes," said the ever-amiable Gopal.

I thought of Akka and wondered about saying

something, but controlled myself. I pointed to the pictures of Krishna instead. "Your favourite god?"

Chanchal assumed a look of deep piety. "I love him. Without him I would be lost. He tells me where to go, holds me up in my hour of sorrow. I can see him. Gopal, tell her how I can see our Lord Krishna."

"Yes, she can see him."

"This morning I woke up feeling sad and when I came down he was sitting right there." She pointed to my chair. "So sweet and calm he looked. He raised his hand and blessed me and then he was gone. Right there he was." She sighed. I shifted nervously at the idea that the god might reappear and I might be sitting on his lap.

"So, tell me about yourself, Anu. Are you liking our town?"

"Yes, it's very interesting."

"And you are happy in the back-house? I gave Suman some pictures to hang on the walls there, to make you feel cheerful. You like it?"

I nodded noncommittally. There were no pictures on my walls. Suman had obviously decided not to hang them up.

"Which one you like better? The cat or the dog?"

"The dog," I lied. I hope she won't decide to come over and visit me in the back-house. I'll have to think of some reason for not having her pictures up on my walls. I must remember to ask Suman about them.

"See, Gopal, I told you, didn't I say she would like the dog better?"

From Gopal's corner came the sound of a gentle snore that sounded oddly like a *yesyes*. I rather like these people.

November 22. Winter has arrived without much notice. It is dark by four o'clock and the sun rises late. I am colder than I have ever been and Suman tells me it will only get worse. The first snow fell today, fat flakes that clung to the bare branches of trees, capping the tightly clenched last buds and falling off the roof of my cabin with thick, soft thumps. I don't mind winter, especially not the beginning, but I've always lived in crowded places. Perhaps I've always been too busy to notice the weather. I wonder how I will like it here in winter in this lonely place where I can actually hear a snowflake fall.

A couple of days ago Suman came over with an armload of comforters, just in case I needed them. When I asked her how she liked winter, she shook her head. "Terrible, it is terrible, Anu. I feel like I might die in this cold. And nothing is growing, oh, that is what kills me." She shuddered. "You must be careful when you go out. I will give you a flashlight to carry with you, and make sure you are always dressed warmly. Also keep a bottle of water and some bars of chocolate."

I laughed. "You make it sound like I'm going on an expedition to the North Pole. Should I take a tent and a stove too?"

She shook her head. "It's not a joke, Anu. Winter here is very cruel."

Part Four

ALL OF THEM

Varsha

December 5th, Hem's birthday! I tiptoed to his room and shook him awake. "Happy Birthday! Look what I have for you."

"What?" Hem stuck his hand out of his warm nest of blankets pretending like he didn't care, but I knew he'd been waiting for my present.

"You have to wake up properly, otherwise you don't get it." I dragged his sheets off completely, leaving him curled up and shivering like an earthworm. "And it's getting late for school. The bus won't wait and Papa will be mad at us."

Hem sat up fast at that. The smell of baking drifted up from the kitchen. A cake, from Mrs. Cooper's recipe, Suman's usual birthday present. She's got no money of her own with which to buy us anything, except for her secret money hidden in her sari. I think she's keeping that to surprise me on my sixteenth birthday. So I pretend I don't know anything about it.

"Open it, Hem, stop being a lazybones." I shook my

parcel under his nose. Hem tore the wrapping. "Careful!" I said.

He opened it more carefully then and unwrapped the notebook. It's not like Anu's, which is a plain old ruled thing, but the kind you might get in a fancy store, with paper that has bits of hayseed and dried flowers in it, stitched together with wool from Suman's mending box. On the cover I'd written in my best script: *For the Snowking.* And below it: *Hem's Book of Snow—From Varsha (his big sister).*

"I made it," I told him. "Every bit of it—the paper too. The flowers are from our own garden. I collected them in the summer and pressed them. I thought of your birthday months ago. Do you like it?"

I always make his presents. Once it was a flight of paper butterflies that floated down on thin strings from the fan in his room right over his bed. I would blow up at them and they would dance for him. For his sixth birthday last year I made windmills and attached them to sticks. Then we raced down the driveway to the gate at the far end, the windmills churning faster and faster.

"It's great!" Hem kissed me all over my face.

"Open it, silly." I pulled it out of his hands and opened it to a pale brown page. "Look—*Aniuk, Aput, Auviq . . .* the Inuit have different names for snow."

"For different *forms* of snow," Hem corrected. He likes to think he knows snow better than anyone in the world.

"Do you like it or not?"

"I love it. It's my favourite present."

I didn't point out that it was probably the only present he would get. Other than something weird from Nick Hutch, that he's found lying around his house—a rusty penknife that can't cut, a set of dentures, some sticky old candy fuzzy with lint from his pocket. And occasionally, I admit, something nice for me: a stone with speckles in different colours, an eagle feather that he had found for us. He, like us, has no money.

But I thought maybe Papa would be in a splendid mood. He might take us for an ice cream treat and buy Hem new clothes too. He is very particular about our clothes. Nothing torn or with holes. No patches or repaired stuff. Only new. "They look at your face and put a price on you," he says. "Clothes make a man." Or, "Beauty lies in the beholder's eye, so make sure you look good."

Akka gave Hem a quarter last night, so he would have it when he woke up this morning. One year she gave him a coin from India, which was kind of useless. On my birthday she gave me a yellowed handkerchief from her suitcase—one she had embroidered herself when she was a girl in India.

Hem took his Snow Book from me and opened another page. This one had a few threads of grass woven into the texture of the paper and a black-and-white picture of blowing snow. My handwriting, black and curly as the hair that hangs down my shoulders, crawled across the top of the page: *Piqsiq*. And below the picture I'd written: *i.e. Snow lifted by the wind i.e. a Blizzard.*

I love using short forms for words like i.e., etc., &, @.
They make me feel as worldly as the school secretary
Jean-Ann who wears high heels and short skirts that she
keeps pulling down over her legs, and who types rapidly
on school letterhead, using i.e. & etc. Sometimes I think
I would like to be a secretary instead of a doctor or a
scientist or a writer. In a city office, one of the tall ones
with big shining windows, where my desk will be right in
the middle so people can see me as soon as they walk in.
There will be a carpet and potted plants all around.

"How do you know what your office will be like
before you have an office?" Hem had asked.

"I have my methods," I had said, assuming a mysterious expression.

"What methods?" he'd said.

"Do I have to tell you everything about me and my
life?"

"Okay, which city is this office in, then?"

I had shrugged. I wasn't sure. Vancouver, maybe, or
Toronto or London or Paris. Paris it would be. "You can
come and live with me," I had offered, feeling magnani-
mous. "I'll get a special car with extra-big doors to drive
you around, the kind with a television screen and music
system and a bar."

Hem was turning the pages of the journal. He found
a drawing of a snow crystal.

"I drew that one. *And* made the book *and* coloured
stuff *and* wrote things. All for the best little boy in the
world."

My brother turned another page and found *Aniuk: Snow for drinking water* accompanied by my sketch of an Eskimo woman chopping at a block of ice. Behind her boiled a pot of water.

"She's too close to the fire." Hem pointed at the woman's elaborate winter jacket decorated with tiny patterns of birds and flowers, and which, I must admit, appeared to trail into the flames behind her. "In fact I think her butt is on fire."

"Is that all you can think of to say, you little brat?" I demanded. "And after all the trouble I took? Well then, give it back!"

"No, I'm sorry, I was teasing!" Hem held the book against his chest and grinned at me. "It's the best present anyone in the whole world has ever given me. And your drawing is as good as Vinci's."

"*Da* Vinci, dumbbell!" I hit him on the shoulder, but I was pleased.

Hem pushed back the blankets and cuddled up to me. "Really truly the best present in the whole wide world. Thank you, Varsha. Where did you find the other pictures?"

"I cut them out from a book."

"One of Papa's books?" Hem squeaked.

I put a finger to my lips. "Shhh! It's our secret, okay?"

"But if he finds out?" Hem was terrified.

"Are you going to tell him? Because I'm not."

"No, no, I won't either." Hem shook his head.

"Now hurry up and get ready for school."

"Can I take it to school and look at it there? For show and tell?"

"Yes, but don't let anyone else touch it, and make sure you give it back to me when we get home so I can hide it."

"Does Mama know?"

"No, silly, it's our secret, yours and mine."

"Can I tell Tree?"

"If you desperately need to, yes."

Bathed and polished in ten and a half minutes flat, Hem put the book into his backpack and we ran down the stairs. Papa was at the table, dressed in a crisp shirt that Suman had ironed exactly the way he likes it, his hair sharply parted on the left side and slick like a seal's skin fresh out of water, his face dark and shining and perfectly shaved. Papa says he approves of neatness and hygiene. He gave me and Hem a critical look each. Clean shirt. Check. Ironed pants. Check. Hair combed. Check. Shoes polished. Check.

"Good morning, children." He smiled. "You both look smart today." I released my pent-up breath in a gasp. I felt taller with pride—praise from Papa is like a piece of jaggery feels in the mouth: delicious and sweet.

"Goodness, Hemu, today you are a whole year smarter." Suman came out of the kitchen with a cake on a blue plate. "I didn't have time to ice it," she said.

Papa clapped and smiled and said in a jolly voice, "Happy, happy birthday, Hem. And here's something from me." He pushed a box towards Hem, who opened it super fast. It was a new pair of woollen gloves and a matching red toque.

"Thank you, Papa!" Hem put his arms around him where he sat beaming at us and kissed him. Then he was jumping up and down from the excitement of having cake for breakfast.

"I'll get the candles," I offered, pulling open the drawer where Suman keeps candles and sewing thread and scissors and other stuff that's used only once in a while.

"So, son, what is your resolution for the year?" Papa asked, still in a good mood, after Hem had blown out his seven candles

"I've decided to get the topmost grades in my class," Hem said, barely lifting his head, "so I can become a doctor. And also to be the best hockey player and the best in my singing class."

"He is already doing so well," Suman said eagerly. "Hem, did you show your Papa your social science test? If Papa has five minutes to see it, of course?"

"Yes, yes. I always have time for my family, Suman, you know that."

"Yes, of course," Suman agreed. She twisted her sari pallu just like I twirl my hair when I'm nervous.

Hem leapt to his feet and pulled his books hastily out of his backpack. *No, no, no, stop, stop, stop.* But Hem was in a hurry. He pulled out his books, quick, quick, quick, before Papa changed his mood, before things exploded, hurry-hurryhurry, show Papa the gold star from Mr. Phillips, that would make him smile, that would make him stroke his moustache and give Hem a hug and a kiss. Out came an English reader, a pencil case, social science book and the Snow Book. Out it fell, flat on its back, the pages open to a large black-and-white photograph of a close-up of a snow crystal on glass. Clumsyclumsyclumsy Hem. I might have known. He is a baby, he never thinks. He can't keep things in. Words spill out of his mouth, secrets spill out of his bag. I might have *known*.

"What's this?" Papa leaned down to pick up the book. Eagle-eyed Papa, nothing gets past him. His mouth stretched so wide a hundred horses could come galloping out.

"Where did you get these pictures from?" he roared. His arm went up like a railway signal and I knew it was about to land on Hem's head, his face, anywhere that hurt. My brother was standing still, terrified, he turned into a pillar like the salt woman in the Bible. Then he was on the floor, I'd pushed him down, and I stood there yelling. "It was me, Papa, I did it. I am sorry. I wanted to give him a special birthday present."

Papa twisted my arm so hard I was sure it would crack in half, but I didn't cry, I didn't make a sound. It would show I am as weak as Suman and that would make Papa even madder than he was.

"I'm sorry, Papa, I am very truly sorry. I will never do such a bad thing again."

He hit me twice across my cheeks and it was as if his hand exploded, hot so hot, right through my skin and into my mouth.

"It's his birthday," Suman moaned, trying to pull me away. "Leave them alone for god's sake. God's sake, please, leave them alone!"

From her room Akka set up a cry as well. "Sumaaan, Sumaaan, Sumaaan. What is going on there? Oh, Sumaaan?" She sounded like a sad bird.

Papa dropped my arm and held his head in his hands. He was sweating. He shook his head. "Why do you make me?"

Suman pushed me away and rushed to Papa's side. She stroked his face as if he was the one who had just been hurt. "It's okay," she murmured. "It's okay." She shook her head at me. "Your poor father is upset, can't you see? Come on, touch his feet and ask for his forgiveness. Come, Varsha." She was giving that look that says I must help her. "Your father is waiting."

"Sorry, Papa," I said again. I bent down and touched his feet, his big, bony feet, ugly, sharp-nailed devil's hooves. I wanted to vomit. I heard Papa sob big tears above my bent head. Then he gathered me into his arms and hugged me close. He smelled of aftershave and hair oil and the camphor from his prayers. I love my Papa and am truly sorry for tearing his book.

"Why do you make your poor Papa so angry, girl?" he asked. "Is this the way a good daughter should behave? Hanh?" He turned to Suman and snapped, "What are you standing there like a fool for? Go get some ice for the child's face." He examined my face anxiously, holding it between his palms and turning it this way and that. "Poor child, poor child. Suman, stupid woman, how long does it take you to get ice? This girl is going to be scarred for life and you slow as a turtle, stupid woman."

Suman returned with the ice tray in one hand and a towel in the other, and Papa handed me to her and wiped his face. He combed his hair in front of the hallway mirror and then he was gone. Thanks to god—not those sly-eyed snickering ones lined up in Papa's prayer room, but the other god, the one who gave me my brother and Suman and Akka.

We assembled silently at the window of the living room and watched him walk down the driveway. He turned and lifted his arm. We waved back.

Suman pressed a sock full of ice gently against my bruised face, kissed me again and again, and said, "Vashi, I am sorry, I am sorry. What should I do? Tell me. Is there anything?"

Useless questions without possible answers. Nothing she can do, all of us know that.

"I hate him," Hem said. "I *hate* him."

I slapped Suman's hand away from my face, angrier with her than with Papa. "I can take it, Mama, I am not a coward like you. And it was my fault anyway. Mine."

"I'll make you gobi parathas when you come home," she said, stroking my hair off my face and dabbing at my cheek with the ice sock. "Hanh? Will that be nice? Shall I?"

Poor stupid Suman, her band-aid for all that hurts us is food. Lots of it. Food is her solace, her refuge, her cure. It's the one thing with which Papa cannot find fault.

"I hate your parathas," I snapped, glad to see the hurt look on her face. "So oily and disgusting. And I smell of them at school. Everyone says so. I smell like curry."

"Then I will make you tomato sandwiches." Tears welled up in her eyes.

"Your sandwiches are worse than your parathas!" I shouted, pressing the ice against my lip. Suman flinched and I was glad again. "And why are *you* crying? He hit me, not you." Then I swung around and glared at Hem, standing there silently, miserably. "What are you standing there for, stupid? Come on, we'll miss the bus."

"Why don't you stay at home today, hanh? I will call the school and say you are both ill." Suman touched my shoulder.

I turned away, pulled on my jacket, gathered my bag, and headed for the door. Hem ran after me, half in and half out of his coat, his toque on wonky, his shoes undone. I spotted my face in the hallway mirror. There was a giant bruise on the left side, it looked like a map.

"Wait for me, I am coming with you also." Suman ran down the driveway after us, waving her ice-filled sock. "If someone asks, don't say anything," she panted when she caught up. "You fell down, that's all."

"Yes, it wouldn't do to tell the truth," I yelled back at her, yanking Hem's arm as we ran. I know it hurts him, but it helps me feel better. "It would ruin our reputation for being the ideal Indian family."

"Vashi, zip your jacket, you will get pneumonia," Suman said, clasping my hand as we stumbled along. "And Hemu, your shoes, your shoes . . ."

It began to snow. Soft, soft, soft it whispered down. Hem stuck out his tongue and caught a plump bud as it dropped from the sky, held out his palm and watched flakes bloom into tears. He was already forgetting the morning drama. It is best to forget things fast in our house. A long memory makes you sad.

The bus appeared like a yellow mirage and I broke away from Suman's pleading clasp. Doors folded back like Japanese fans, Mr. Wilcox waved at us and we climbed in, panting out powder-puff breaths, the kind that stay in the air for a second before vanishing.

"Hey, Varsha, what happened to your face? Walked into a door, did you?" Mr. Wilcox asked, peering at me.

"Fell down the stairs," I said.

"She bumped into a wall," Hem said at the exact same moment. A heartbeat's pause. Will Mr. Wilcox notice? Will he guess? Does he know? And has he too taken a vow of silence like the rest of our town?

"And then I fell down the stairs," I said. My whole head hurt. "Bumped into a wall and fell down the stairs." *Right into my Papa's fist.*

"Oh yeah? Gotta look where you're going, kiddo. Grab a seat, now. Don't want you falling down and getting hurt all over again, do we?"

I passed Nick Hutch to get to Varsha's Seat at the back of the bus, and he gave me a sympathetic look. He knew. All the kids at school know, the teachers too. The whole world knows, but nobody says a thing.

When I got to school, I kicked Mathew Firth in the shin for saying my face looked like it was punched. I did it even though I knew the principal would call Papa and complain about how terrible I am and then when we got home Papa would punish me some more. All this I knew would *happen-ay-happen*, as Akka says. But in that sweet moment when I saw Mathew's face crumple into pain, when I saw his tears, I felt *good*.

Anu's Notebook

December 5. Sounds carry more easily now, and today I heard raised voices as I passed the house on my way out. I thought I heard them before a couple of times, but I wasn't sure. Perhaps it's Varsha being a teenager and driving her dad crazy with her insolence. Perhaps Vikram can't find his socks and is hollering for them the way my father used to do. The only difference was that my mother, unlike Suman, would not rush around the house in a panic trying to find a matching pair of socks for her lord and master. She would continue doing whatever it was she was doing, and when my father hollered some more, she would say, "So wear my socks, nobody's going to check under your trousers, are they?"

This morning, however, heading out for my morning walk on the now crisp snow, I did hear someone weeping hard, and then Vikram shouting. I paused, uneasy, wondering whether to check, changed my mind and carried on. By the time I returned, everything was quiet again. I caught a glimpse of Suman through the kitchen window, doing her thing, cooking up a storm, which I could smell almost all the way to my cottage. She came over, as usual, a little after noon, with my lunch and a hefty slice of chocolate cake.

"Hemu's birthday," she said, before I could ask what the occasion was. She looked tired and tense. I wondered if it had something to do with the sounds I'd heard earlier.

"Oh, I wish I'd known," I said. "I would have got him a present. How old is he?"

"Seven. And no, you must not waste your money with presents and all."

"Why not? It's my money. What do you think he'd like? A board game? A T-shirt? What's his favourite colour?"

To my astonishment, Suman began to sob.

"What is it? Did I say something I shouldn't have?" I asked, alarmed.

"No, no, you are so kind, so kind," she whispered through her tears. I held out my hands and she clutched them, drawing them to her cheek.

I made her sit in the single dining chair, handed her some tissues, which she didn't really need since she mopped her face with the end of her sari. I waited until she had herself under control and asked, "Suman, now tell me honestly, is everything okay with you at home?"

She gave me a panicked look and seemed about to burst into tears again. "Yes, why are you asking? Did anyone say anything to you?"

"No, but I heard somebody crying this morning, before the kids left for school. And in the past few months too, I've thought I heard shouting from your house sometimes. What's going on?"

"You can hear *everything*?" She got to her feet and started to back out of the cottage. "What did you hear?"

"No, I can't hear everything, don't be silly. Only a few times when I was passing your house, I thought I might have heard sounds of, you know, crying and Vikram was shouting . . ."

By now Suman was looking so upset I wished I hadn't brought up any of this. But I had, and I was determined to get to the bottom of whatever is going on in that house. "Is there something wrong? Is Varsha in trouble?"

"Why? Did she tell you something? Did they say something in town?"

"No. Nobody said anything. Calm down. She's a teenager, and they get into all kinds of stuff. So I thought, maybe—"

"I have to go. Please don't tell. I am sorry I cried. No need for a present. It is okay."

"Please, Suman. If there is something wrong, maybe I can help. And if it is Varsha, it's only a phase. She'll get over it. I remember being pretty obnoxious myself, at that age." I felt like a blabbering fool, giving the woman tips on child-rearing without knowing a goddamn thing about it. "So tell me. What's wrong?"

Suman gathered herself and shook her head. "There is nothing. I am telling you. This weather makes me feel depressed, that's all." She opened the door and nodded at me a couple of times. "That's all," she said again. "The weather."

I watched her wade through the thickening carpet of snow. She was lying. I know.

January 6, 1980. Back from my much-needed break. It was good to see the family. Even my brother—we didn't quarrel once. Mummy was still hanging in there. Met up with Carole and gave all the Dharma gossip. Got a pedicure and a much-needed haircut. Partied the New Year in, drank myself silly. Surprisingly I don't mind being back here. I'm determined to get at least five stories done by spring. I went over to the Dharmas with some pastries from my favourite place in Vancouver but was more or less shooed away from their door.

Hemant

Varsha says I'm a blabbermouth. It's my genes she says. Those are a different kind of genes. She says I have Akka's genes and Akka likes talking a lot. There's nothing anyone can do about their genes. I can't help it—everything comes out when I'm scared and my brain stops working.

Like on my birthday when the Snow Book came out of my bag, and Papa hit Varsha for tearing his book to make it for me, and then she kicked a boy in school and then the principal called Papa and Mama in to talk to them about it after which she was in BIG trouble again. I said sorry and kissed her all over her face but my sister is brave and good and she said not to worry, it wasn't really my fault and if she didn't have me she didn't know what she would do.

And then I got her into trouble again yesterday after that trip to buy a purple lollipop from Mr. Johnson's store. It was a secret and I wasn't to tell anyone. But it fell out of my mouth before I could think. I told Papa we went to Mr. Johnson's store. We are not to go to their store. *Ever.* Papa says he would know if we did. He says Mr. Johnson is a PERVERT.

But Akka gave me a quarter for my birthday and said to get myself the nicest thing I could imagine. I kept it and kept it, because I couldn't think what *was* the nicest thing. Then I thought about a giant lollipop and so after school Varsha took me across the road to Mr. Johnson's store.

"We have five minutes before the bus gets to the school gates, Hem. So hurry up, okay?" Varsha pushed open the door of the shop and bells jingled to let Mr. Johnson know that somebody was coming in.

"Papa will be mad at us if he finds out," I whispered, tugging at Varsha's skirt.

"He won't find out. Unless we miss the bus. So hurry up."

I went up to the counter to see which colour lollipop I liked and Mr. Johnson leaned over and patted my head. "Got your allowance, did you, young man?" he asked.

"No sir, it's my grandma's birthday present," I said proudly, showing him my quarter.

"Birthday, eh? How old are you, son?"

"Seven."

"Well then, happy birthday and guess what, you get to pick a lollipop for free! And keep the quarter for next time."

We ran back across the road and in a few minutes the bus was there. I was happier than happy. I had a lollipop I licked as hard as I could so it would be done by the time we got home, and I still had my quarter for another lolli-pop. Maybe I would buy one for Varsha next time.

I snuggled close to her. She looked down at me and said, "Your mouth is all purple. You look like a clown. We'd better wipe it off or Papa will know." She spat on some tissue and wiped my lips hard. It hurt but some of the purple went away and I licked my lips the rest of the way so the rest of the colour would go away too.

By the time the bus stopped at Fir Tree Lane my lips were all clean, my sister checked.

. We ploughed through the snow to where Mama was waiting for us in a long black puffy coat. She was wearing a red sari which peeked out from under her coat. Under the sari I knew she was wearing flannel pyjamas. Otherwise the wind would go up and freeze her legs to death. Akka told Papa not to be such a lunatic stick-in-the-mud and force Mama into saris in winter. But Papa said she was his wife and he would decide what she was to wear. And that was that.

Mama's face was wrapped in a pink and green muffler. I could see only her eyes. She carried a flashlight in one hand and the satchel on her shoulder like always. In it she had rolled-up parathas, chocolate bars, some cookies, bottles of water. And in another bag two extra jackets for us, just in case we forgot ours at school. Mama is terrified of the cold and comes armed to the teeth against it.

I flung myself at her, hugging her tight, and she buried her face in my hair.

"Oof, what a smelly child!" she said. "And why aren't

you wearing your hat? You will catch cold, you know."
She held out a hand for me. "Safety in numbers," she said
as we trudged off down the lane. She always says the same
things every day.

"Papa's home early," Mama said after a while.

I looked at Mama's half-hidden face, checking to see
if she had black eyes.

"What is it?" Mama's voice was muffled by the scarf.
"Why are you both so quiet?"

"Why?" Varsha demanded.

"Why what?" Mama was holding my hand tight.

"Don't pretend, Mama," Varsha said sternly. "Why is
he home already?"

Mama stopped walking, so I almost fell. "They closed
the mill early today."

"Is he in a bad mood?" I asked.

"Did he lose his job?" Varsha wanted to know. In
school they said everyone in town was losing their jobs
one by one. The mill was in the red. Like it was bleeding
to death maybe. Mama said that's why we had to rent out
the back-house to Anu. To give us an INCOME in case
Papa's job ended.

"He hasn't said."

"There's a blizzard expected today," I called out.
I climbed a snowbank and sank nearly up to my armpits.

"A blizzard? It wasn't in the news, was it?" Mama
asked.

"I can smell it." That made me sound important, and
we could stop talking about Papa. Maybe the blizzard

would carry us away across the lake, over the mountains, somewhere nice and safe.

"Don't believe him, Mama," Varsha said. "They announced it on the radio this afternoon. Sudden storm coming up they said. It's been hiding behind the mountains."

Like a wolf. Waiting for its prey. Who would die this winter? The snow here always gets at least one person every year. Once it was my grandfather, Mr. J.K. Dharma.

"Come on then, stop dawdling," Mama said. "We don't want to get caught in the storm, do we?"

"We could die of HYPOTHERMIA," I added, picking up a handful of snow and throwing it at my sister. We ran ahead of Mama. I was laughing and shouting.

"Wait for me!" she called. "Wait for me!" But I think it's not easy to run in a sari in the snow.

Then I saw that the sky had turned grey all around us and was mixed up with the ground. There was no horizon. I couldn't see where the road ended and the frozen lake began. The mountains had vanished in the snow. I counted steps in my head, looking down at my feet, sometimes back to spot the holes that my boots had left behind, and when I finished counting there was our gate pressed open by the snow. Our house was crouching like a big fat cat, its roof white, giant heaps of snow all around it. The front light was a shiny golden bead over the door. And behind the door waited Papa. Waited for us to come home to him.

He opened the door and I saw him begin to grow

into a giant. His head puffed up, his eyes swelled into monster-sized rounds, his arms, his legs, his toes, his nose, all stretched out this way and that. And as he grew larger the three of us grew tinier. We became little ants, or sparrows he could smash in a second.

I love him because he is my Papa. I know he hits us because he loves us, and it's his duty to turn us into the best children in the world, into children he can be proud of. He found out about our trip to the store. Like he said he would. He has eyes all over his head. He is like god. He spotted my purple tongue and then he pointed out a smudge of purple lollipop on my sweater.

"You ate something nice, son?" he asked in his kind Papa voice.

I said, "Yes Papa, a giant lollipop." I nodded eagerly.

"Was it delicious then, son? Did your teacher give it to you?"

"Oh no, it was Mr. Johnson. He gave it to me for free and Varsha said it was okay for me to take it and I said thank you to Mr. Johnson, I did, Papa." Blab blab blab.

Our father called us to the room full of books belonging to his dear dead father Mr. J.K. Dharma, which we are not to touch, ever.

Varsha held my hand, squeezing hard to let me know I was not to be afraid. She stared at Papa straight in the eye, even though she's a tiny thing, just like Mama.

Papa's belt coiled out of his hand like a snake, not the cloth one which doesn't hurt as much but the leather one which does.

He whipped Varsha first then me. Little hills and flowers of blood came up on our legs.

Mama started to cry and begged him to leave us alone.

Then in the middle of it all the doorbell rang. That got Papa to stop.

"Suman? Are you okay?" It was Anu. More ringing.

Papa glared at Mama and whispered, "Why is she here at this time? Does she come over often?" Our business is our business, nobody else's.

"No, she doesn't, she doesn't. I don't know what she wants."

"You take these two upstairs. I'll deal with her," Papa said.

The knob rattled and Anu called out again, "Is everything okay? Suman? Akka?"

Mama rushed us up the stairs. No noise, she whispered, no noise. We went into her room and she shut the door. Down below we heard voices and then Anu was gone and Papa was coming up the stairs. The door opened and he was there. "Nosy Parker," he said. "I am not sure it's such a good idea to have her around." He looked sharply at Mama. "Does she do that when I am not here?"

"Do what?" Mama looked confused and scared.

"Come to the house?"

"No, I hardly see her. I think she is busy writing her book," Mama said.

"Are you sure?" Papa caught Mama by the chin like

she was a child and turned her face up so he could look
closely at her.

"No. I mean yes. I mean yes I am sure. Ask Akka if
you want," Mama said.

There was a long silence and then Papa moved away
from my Mama. "Okay," he said. "Okay."

And then Mama had to go down to make dinner and
we had to go to our rooms to do our homework and later
still, when the house was quiet, I could hear Varsha crying
in her room. It was my fault. I wished I was not a blabbermouth, I wished I had not eaten a purple lollipop.
Good thing it was winter and our legs would be covered
up. And Mama would say to us as we walked to the bus
stop, don't tell anyone, okay? No one at all. On my head,
promise on my head, or I will die and you will not have
me with you any longer. Nobody must know what
happens inside our house. It's like hanging out your dirty
underwear in the public square Mama says. In summer
when she hangs out our underwear to dry she covers
them with towels so nobody, not even the sparrows, can
see them sitting there quiet as mice, like us. Promise,
Mama. Promise, Varsha. I won't tell. Otherwise I'll go to
hell. Otherwise people will think bad things about us.

Anu's Notebook

January 24. Yesterday evening, trudging back to my cottage after a trip to town, I heard an almighty racket going on in the Dharma house again—crying, shouting, the works. Somebody, it sounded like Suman, was pleading or wailing, I couldn't be sure. I hesitated— was it any of my business to interfere? Decided to check anyway, in case something was really wrong, like maybe Akka was dead. The house was sparsely lit as usual. Suman tells me Vikram doesn't like wasting electricity. If there's nobody in a room, the lights are turned off. The light over the front door stays on all night. I pulled my jacket about me and walked through ankle-deep snow and rang the bell. Silence descended abruptly. I waited, shivering as the frigid wind bit at my face, making my eyes water, and rang again. This time I heard footsteps approaching and Vikram opened the door, plainly annoyed.

"Anu. What can I do for you?" he asked, wedging his body in the doorway so that I couldn't see inside.

"Nothing, I just heard some noises, and was wondering . . . Is everything okay?"

"Yes, why shouldn't it be?"

"Well, it sounded like someone was crying and shouting and, well, I got worried. I thought maybe Akka . . ."

"Probably the radio. Didn't realize it was so loud, sorry." Vikram smiled. "Is there anything else?"

"No, no, I should be apologizing for disturbing you." I backed away, feeling stupid.

Another cordial smile from Vikram and then the door was shut. I walked slowly back to my cottage, thinking, he's lying, it was definitely not the radio I heard. Stop it, Anu. Stop poking your nose into everything. None of your business. You are just a tenant. Nevertheless, the feeling of unease stays with me. I can't in all conscience do nothing if Vikram is bashing up his family. But I am not sure what I should be doing. Would things turn worse for Suman if I interfered?

Then, this morning, I bumped into the three of them—Suman, Varsha and Hemant—on their way to the bus stop. Varsha's face was all puffy and bruised.

"Hello! What on earth happened to you?" I was genuinely concerned. She looked terrible.

"Nothing," they all said in unison, mother and two kids.

"Doesn't look like nothing to me," I remarked.

They went quiet, all of them. Suman looked positively terrified. Then Varsha found her voice and said, "I got into a fight with a guy at school yesterday. That's all."

"You got beaten by somebody at school? Bloody bullies! Did you complain?"

Varsha shrugged. "I can deal with it. Bye, we're going to miss the bus."

I don't believe a word of it. Now I think about it, in the six months I've been here, I've noticed bruises on the children—mostly on their legs. I just assumed they were normal scrapes and bumps. Now I'm beginning to connect the dots: the shouting, the bruises, the fear. Does he hit Suman too? Or is it only the kids? Does Akka know? How can she not? She lives in the same house. My respect for the old woman descends several notches. How does she sit there and watch her son beat up his wife and kids? The more I think about it, the more agitated I get. I might not like Varsha or Hemant very much, but they are children. Maybe I should report Vikram to the police.

"He hits them, doesn't he?" I asked Suman. I was waiting for her at the gate, when she got back from dropping the kids off at the bus stop. "And you? Does he do it to you too?"

She gave me an evasive look and pushed past me, refusing to look at me again or say anything. I trailed after her. When we got to the house, she wouldn't let me in.

"Please, I have many things to do today. Very busy. I cannot talk now."

"Does he hit you too, Suman? You can tell me, you know. We can report it, it's not right. I could help if you need. Or maybe I could speak to Vikram? He might stop whatever it is he's doing if he realizes I know."

A look of horror crept across her face. "No, no, please don't say anything to him. He will . . ." She stopped and composed herself. "There is nothing wrong. Please leave. I am busy. Varsha was rushing down the stairs and fell, that is all. Why are you making a big drama about it all?"

"She said she was in a fight, Suman. You guys need to get your lies straight if you want me to believe you."

"I am not lying. She was in a fight and they pushed her down the stairs. I have forgotten. There are bad children in her school."

She didn't bring me any lunch this afternoon. Am I being punished or is she avoiding me? I think it's the latter—Suman does not seem the kind of person who could punish anybody. Then, just before supper, she showed up with an invitation from Vikram to join them for dinner on Saturday next week. She was all excited about it; the events of this morning seemed all forgotten.

"You must dress nicely," she said. "We are inviting Gopal and Chanchal. Remember, I told you about them?"

I was taken aback. Wonder why Vikram is turning so cordial all of a sudden. Does it have anything to do with my knock on their door last night or my questions this morning?

"You can come? Yes? Vikram insisted that we must have you over. We wanted to do this before, but somehow . . ." She tailed off and gave me one of her imploring looks.

"Yes, yes, of course, that would be lovely. I'll be there. It isn't as if I have an appointment book full of things to do, either!" I was trying to make her smile her sweet smile but wasn't successful. "By the way, I meant to tell you, I met Chanchal and Gopal in town yesterday and they kindly invited me home for tea and some yummy cookie thing—naan khatai, I think it was called. Characters, both of them. But really nice, I thought."

I've never seen Vikram interacting with his family or any friends, and I'm curious. It's so odd that I never even bump into him, although I know he's at home on Fridays as well as weekends lately. Akka told me it was because of cutbacks at the lumber mill.

"Dress nicely? But I don't have any fancy clothes. Will a pair of clean trousers and a shirt do?"

"You don't wear saris?" Suman asked. "You are from India, no?"

"Well, my parents are. And yes, I do wear saris occasionally and not very comfortably, but right now I don't have any with me. So it will have to be trousers and a blouse, I'm afraid. I promise to look good, not to worry."

"It's okay. It's a family dinner and family friends. Do you want me to make anything special? Vikram said to ask."

He's really laying it on, I thought. I must have stirred things up. I assured Suman that anything she made was manna from heaven as far as I was concerned. Even her plain rice tasted better than the fancy stuff you can eat in posh restaurants. She smiled, pleased, and hurried away as fast as she could through the snow which had started falling again.

January 25. I had more visitors today—the children this time. I was outside, smoking peacefully, enjoying the crisp air, the brilliant sunshine, when I heard footsteps crunching towards me.

"Hi, Anu Aunty, how are you?" Varsha called, waving.

I almost swallowed my cigarette from shock. Anu *Aunty*! And smiles instead of scowls! What is going on?

"Oh, you startled me," I remarked. The bruises on Varsha's face have faded a bit. They aren't as bad as they were yesterday.

"Sorry, we just came by to apologize for our rudeness," she said.

"Yes, apologize," the little echo added.

"Nothing to apologize for. You weren't rude at all. Your face looks pretty beaten up. Are you better now?"

"Yes, yes I am. I had a really bad fall down the stairs, you know, three guys pushed me. Big guys," Varsha said.

"Oh really?" It looks like the entire family has closed ranks and is insisting on the same fib.

"You don't believe me?" she said challengingly, more like her usual self. "What do you think happened to me then?"

I thought it might be an opening. "You tell me. I wouldn't know what goes on inside your house. Would you like to tell me?"

"Inside our house? I got hurt at school."

"We love our Papa," little Hem piped up, without any prompting from Big Sister, and apropos nothing.

She gave him a quick nudge and laughed. "He's such a silly-billy. Of course we love Papa and Mama and Akka—they are our family. Just like you love your family, I suppose. Mama said you have a brother and two nephews around my age. Do you love them?"

"I guess, most of the time, when they're behaving themselves," I said, blowing smoke into the cold air. Where are we going with this conversation? I wondered.

"You shouldn't smoke, it's bad for your health," Varsha said. "You can get lung cancer."

"Yeah, I know, Miss Smarty-pants." I grinned at her.

She grinned back, her whole face lightening. I think she could be nice if she tried. "Then why are you doing it?"

"Because I enjoy it, that's why," I said. "Don't you ever do anything because it makes you feel good?"

"Not if it's bad. My Papa would be upset." Her voice was prim again, her frown back.

I tried again. "Hey, Hemant, did you like the T-shirt I gave you for your birthday? You never said anything. Did it fit?"

"Yes, he loved it," Varsha said.

"Doesn't your brother have a voice? Hmm?"

Varsha nudged Hem. "Tell her how much you loved it, Hem."

"I loved it," the boy repeated obediently. "Thank you very much, Aunty Anu." But then he surprised me. "What are you writing about? Mama said you were looking for stories. Have you found any?"

"Maybe, I'm not sure," I said cautiously. Have they been reading my notebook in my absence? I must remember to carry it with me when I leave the cottage. "I'm just making notes at the moment. Nothing definite."

"Are you writing about us?" he piped up. No prompting from his sister. Perhaps the little man is developing a mind of his own.

"Do you want me to write about you?" I asked, smiling at him.

Before he could respond, his sister had decided our little meeting was done. She was probably exhausted from being nice to me. She took his arm and started back to the house, which looked warm and inviting with golden light filling the windows.

"See you then, Anu," she said. "Make sure you don't drop your cigarette butt on the ground. It will look horrid in the spring when the snow melts."

"Hey! What happened to Anu Aunty?" I called after them, but they didn't look back, either of them, and I was left alone in the gathering dusk.

I am still mulling over this unexpected visit and sudden short burst of pleasantry. What did they really want to find out?

January 30. Met Chanchal again, minus Gopal. He was apparently busy building a bird feeder back at the house. "Very kind man," Chanchal explained. "It breaks his heart that poor birdies have no food in winter. So."

This time I dragged her to Bradford's café for a chat. I needed to talk to her about the Dharmas. She's known them far longer than me; she would have a better sense of what, if anything, is going on there.

"So, I hear you're coming over to dinner next week?" I started.

"Yes, it is a long time. Vikram is very busy. I will be happy to see them all."

I decided to get to the point. "Chanchal, I want to ask you. You know them well. Is there something wrong in that house?"

Chanchal's expressive face looked uncomfortable. "Wrong? What do you mean?"

"I mean, does Vikram beat his kids?"

Chanchal shrugged. "I don't know all this. Sometimes children can be bad. A spanking won't hurt them. Your mother-father never got angry with you?"

"And how about Suman? Does he hit her too?"

She stared at me. Her face became shuttered. "These matters are between husband and wife."

"But sometimes it is your job as a friend to intervene."
She was silent.

"Have you heard anything about this? You've been in this town a long time. You've known this family for years. Gopal is an old friend of Vikram's."

Chanchal shook her head. "Nobody is saying any-thing to me. I don't know. Now I must leave. No time for tea. Gopal will be worried if I don't come home on time." She gathered up her bags and hesitated. "What if it is true? Can you do anything? Nobody has complained, no? How to do anything if nobody complains? *What* to do?"

Hemant

Varsha and me read Anu's notebook a little bit when she was in town. She wrote mean things about us. She called me REPULSIVE which means yukky as a dead frog. Varsha said. I am *not* a dead frog. I am a *person*.

She also wrote that Papa is a bad man who beats us. She wrote that Akka killed our grandpa. "She is lying," I said to Varsha. "Akka is *good*." I didn't know what I should say about Papa, I get mixed up when I think about him so I kept quiet. "Our Akka would never do such a thing, would she Varsha? Would she?"

But Varsha shook her head and said our grandfather was a drunkard. He had hurt our Akka and disgraced our family, and he deserved to die. She said if Akka did kill him she was a real smarty-pants the way she got rid of him. She said it was murder without any EVIDENCE and she will be a lawyer one day so she knows all about crime and stuff. Anu wrote that our grandfather became a pillar of ice. Which is what Akka tells us, but she laughs when she tells us.

"How do you become a pillar of ice?" I asked Varsha.

"It's a figure of speech, stupid." She slapped the side of my head, not gently like she does when she loves me but hard so it stung.

I know my sister is annoyed with me because I'm beginning to like Anu. She bought me a brand new T-shirt for my birthday. She brings cakes from the bakery in town and she doesn't mind sitting with Akka when Mama fetches us from the bus stop. I think she's nice. She asked my sister when her birthday was, but Varsha said it was none of her business. The T-shirt was a cheap way to buy my affections, she said. Her Snow Book was much harder to make. Plus she'd SUFFERED a beating from Papa for my sake. She would do anything for my sake. Would I?

"Yes, yes!" I said, hugging my sister. I felt bad about hurting her feelings. Also I didn't like Anu anymore because she called me REPULSIVE.

"Then you must cut up the T-shirt Anu gave you and throw it away."

I didn't want to. I liked it.

"You said you would do anything for my sake. Do you want to break my heart?"

I wanted wanted *wanted* to keep my T-shirt.

"If you break my heart I will be dead," Varsha said. "Then my ghost will come and cry in your room every night. What will you do then, Hem? What will you do?"

So I threw my birthday present in the garbage like my sister said because I didn't want her to die of a broken heart and come back as a ghost to haunt me. I was not to smile or be friends with Anu either, Varsha said. She was a crook and she was going to steal our Mama from under our noses and then where would we be?

"How do you know she is going to?" I asked Varsha.

"She wrote it in her book, silly. Don't you remember?"

"Yes, but she told Mama she was writing a *story*, not real things. Maybe it was only a story. Mama would never leave us. She loves us more than the whole wide world."

"It was real. It's called an autobiographical story."

I still didn't believe her, but I kept quiet because I didn't want her to get mad at me.

Anu's Notebook

February 1. Today I decided to corner Suman in her own territory—the kitchen of the main house. Through the bare trees and rattling branches, the main house is more visible now and it looks very pretty, hunkered down in the whiteness, small icicles dripping down from the rim of the roof. Snow is heaped up all around except for a narrow path that Vikram has cleared from my door to the house, around the house, and on to the gate. Yet even as I walked, it began to snow again and the path became less and less distinct. Vikram is fastidious about clearing that pathway most of the time, but it's hard for him to keep up. I watch him sometimes with the snow blower, in his blue jacket, ploughing through the snow, pausing now and again to swipe a mittened paw across his nose, and wonder how he looks so harmless.

The wind groaned in the trees. A branch cracked and fell just ahead of me. My heart jumped—I appreciate nature in all its naked glory, but lately, especially after that last snowstorm, it's starting to get to me. If I fell, how

long before I am found lying in the snow? I am beginning
to understand why Suman carries all kinds of emergency
supplies in her bag on that walk to the bus stop to pick up
her kids. I now understand her winter paranoia. The solitude, the isolation, the silence—it's all nerve-racking,
especially at night alone in my cottage, which is more
or less roof-deep in the white stuff. Far overhead the
sun struggles to make its presence felt, casting a pallid
yellow light over the landscape. Yesterday morning
when I forced myself to head off for my daily walk, to
keep my energy levels up, to avoid being swallowed up by
this beast called winter, I could barely make out where
anything was—the field turning into the road into the
lake into the shrubs and distant mountains, all outlines
erased by the descending whiteness.

The weather report is calling for another major storm
tonight and the sky and the earth have merged into a
steely sameness. The thought of living through this for
the next six months depresses me. What was I thinking
of when I signed my wretched lease for an entire year?
The silence which seemed so idyllic in summer is now a
nightmare. And the frigging cold—I don't remember
cold being *this* cold!

I tapped on the kitchen window and Suman looked
up, startled, from her cooking. She smiled when she saw it
was me and opened the door. "What are you doing here,
Anu? I would have come later on. I have made such tasty
rasam today. Perfect for this cold weather, you know."

"Does he hit you too, Suman?" I asked her, straight

off the bat. I didn't want to give her time to consider her response. "The way he beats your children? And don't tell me he doesn't—I've seen those bruises and they don't come from falling down the stairs or tripping on shoes. Why are you lying? Why are you protecting him?"

She backed away, her face sinking into familiar lines of anxiety. "I wasn't lying," she said at last, wearily. "He doesn't beat me, not really."

"Oh? Then what does he do? How come everybody in this house, including you, is so clumsy? Falling all the time? Give me a break, Suman. I'm not a fool."

"Shh, stop talking so loudly. She will hear."

"Who? Akka? Well, she should be ashamed of herself, letting her son do this to you. I would have thought she knew better!"

"No, no, Varsha. She is at home with flu. She is sleeping upstairs. Please go away now." Suman pushed me towards the door.

"No, I won't. And if you don't tell me the truth, I'm going up there to wake up that girl and drag it out of her. You mustn't be afraid. You can get help. I can help you. Please."

Suman gave me a bitter look. "You don't know anything," she said in a low voice, turning away from me. "You don't know how it is to be alone, to be without any money or anywhere to go for help. Yes, I lied about what he does to me, but it was only a partial lie. He doesn't raise his hand to me the way he does with the children. Not anymore. Not after I lost my baby."

"You lost your baby? I'm sorry, Suman. What happened?"

She shook her head.

"Was it his fault? It was, wasn't it?"

Silence again.

"Okay, you said he doesn't hit you anymore. But he does hurt you, I know. What does he do? Tell me."

"Pushes me sometimes, or squeezes my arm so hard I can feel his fingers on them for an entire week. He isn't a bad man, really. He doesn't mean to hurt us. You must understand."

I don't understand at all. I am angry at the excuses.

"He punishes me in other ways," Suman continued. "No money in the bank account that I am allowed to use, so I have to pay at the grocery store with handfuls of pennies and nickels and dimes. Calling me stupid, criticizing everything I do, even my food. My food—anyone can see how good I am in the kitchen, but you've never had to ask anyone for money like a beggar every day, have you? Even to buy sanitary napkins? Or a chocolate candy? No, you haven't. So how would you understand? Vikram is good at that sort of subtle humiliation. His violence is more hurtful because nobody can see it. You can't put ointment or a cold pack on or eat a Tylenol to take away those marks and that pain. His attacks, they go for the root of your being, kill your self-respect, your idea of who you are, take away your sense of balance. That's why we are always falling, we have no sense of balance in this

house. Vikram calls me a fool and I've *become* one. I hate
how easily I've given in. I thought, for a while, that if
I loved him enough he would stop. But it doesn't work
that way. It could only be the kind of love a prisoner
feels for her guard." She stopped, drew a harsh breath
and turned to look at me. "There," she said quite calmly,
no tears. "There, I've told you. Can you still help me?
Hanh? Can you?"

I nodded. "Yes, I can. I will, I promise you. Have you
never told anyone all this? Surely somebody would have
done something. I can't believe everybody in this town is
indifferent. Don't you have any friends?"

"No, I don't. I was ashamed to tell anyone. And
anyway, what could I have done without money or a
passport? He has hidden my passport so I can't leave.
Even now, you say you can help me, but where do I get
a passport from?"

"We will deal with the passport thing later. It's probably expired anyway. You can say you lost it. But that can
come later. To begin with, let's get you out of here. After
that, you get in touch with my lawyer. Here, I brought
you her address and phone number. Keep it until you
decide. If you agree, I'll phone her for you and fix an
appointment, okay? And I can lend you money to tide
you over until you find your feet. Yes?"

"No. I don't know. I won't be able to manage."

"Yes you will, Suman, you just need to set your mind
to it. It's not right. Not for you, not for those kids. Do
you want them to end up like you?"

"No," she whispered. She tucked the piece of paper inside her pocket. "But Varsha won't come, she loves her father. I am not really her mother, you know, and how can I take Hemant away from his father? It is not right. No, I can't do it. You must leave now. If Varsha comes down, she will be upset. She must not know. She will be so hurt."

"Well then, you will have to leave her behind, nothing to be done about that. But you, and Hemant—think of him at least, Suman. You've got to leave."

"Who's leaving?" Varsha materialized near the kitchen door silently. I jumped then, in a kind of fear myself. How much did she hear, the little sneak? "What is she doing here? Mama, are you going somewhere?"

"No, I am," I said. "I'm sick of this weather. I don't know if I can take it anymore." I smiled at her, ignored the ferocious scowl. The Aunty Anu business has faded right out of her system—the girl is back to being her nasty little self. "I hear you're not well. Did you catch something at school?"

"Yes, you better leave, you might catch it too," she said. "And since you are old, it might kill you."

Brat! She went up to Suman, curved an arm possessively around her waist and dropped her head onto her shoulder. "Mama, I feel terrible," she pouted, giving a sad little sniff. "I think I have a fever. Here, feel my head."

Suman avoided looking at me and placed her palm on Varsha's forehead. I caught the girl's eye and got the feeling she had heard our entire conversation. It makes

me uneasy. I wonder what she will do with the knowledge—tell Vikram? So what if she does? He can't touch
me. But I think of what he could do to Suman and am
worried. I know I must make one more attempt to persuade Suman to leave. If that doesn't work, what do I do?
If she won't help herself, can anybody help her?

Varsha

A horrid day. I was sick with the flu and Suman was planning to go away. I heard her say so to Anu. She was going to take my brother with her but not me. She told Anu I'm not hers. But *she* is mine, and Hem too. He's most definitely mine. *I* saw him first.

It was all Anu's fault. She was the one influencing my stepmother. She was the one messing with my family. Suman is weak, she doesn't know what she's doing.

"Are you going somewhere, Mama?" I asked, holding her close. I am almost as tall as her. A nerve in her soft neck jumped against my cheek.

"No, no, where would I go without you and Hem?" she lied.

"I heard Anu and you talking, Mama," I said. Again her pulse leaped against my cheek.

"She was talking about her story, that's all," Suman said. She unwrapped my arms from around her waist and moved away.

Liar liar lipstick, borne on a broomstick. I hoped the

broomstick broke and gave her a good poke, a hard, painful poke. I was mad at her. I *am* mad at her. I love her like she is really my mother, even though she is nowhere near as beautiful or as smart. But she's going to take my brother and leave us like Mom did. I am madder than mad.

"Here, some hot tea with honey." Suman gave me a steaming mug. Who will take care of me if she leaves? Who will stop Papa from beating the shit out of me? Who will wash my hair on Sunday mornings and make chocolate cake on my birthday? I cannot let her go.

She gave me a worried look and was about to say something when we both heard a funny noise.

"Did you hear that?" Suman asked. "Was that your grandmother?" She ran out of the kitchen, hurrying to Akka's room with me behind her. Akka was slumped down in her chair, going *rrr-rrr-rrr* like an engine which won't start up. Her mouth was twisted sideways.

"Oh no," Suman cried. "Something is wrong with her." We leaned over Akka, so old and beloved, and she stopped going *rrr-rrr* for a few seconds to mutter something. Her voice sounded like a rusty gate creaking open after a thousand years, and then she fell silent. Her dry breath rustled through her ancient lungs like dead leaves. Only the fingers of her left hand moved in a funny little dance. I started to cry even though I know that tears are a sign of weakness. But this was my beloved gran, my Akka, and she was going to die, I could feel it in the air around her.

She was going to die and Suman was leaving with my brother. They were all leaving me.

"Go phone 911, quick, we need to call the ambulance," Suman said, pushing me out of the room. It felt like that day seven years ago when Hemant was born. Only this was a departure and that was an arrival.

"Then I must phone Papa and let him know, and you go and get Anu," Suman said. She was running back and forth. What will she do on her own without me or Papa to take care of her, has she thought about that?

"Why do I have to get Anu?" I wanted to know.

"Because I am going with Akka to the hospital and you can't stay alone at home."

I didn't want that meddling bitch here, but it was not the time to create a fuss. I called 911, and we waited and waited forever, but perhaps it was only fifteen minutes. Then I went and got Anu.

We watched them load my grandmother into the dark hollow of the van, and watched Suman clamber in after her. Anu stood beside me in her black parka, shivering slightly. I hate her. She tried to put her arm around my shoulder but I moved away. Her fault. Everything is her fault.

"I am sorry," Anu said. The traitor. The thief. "I hope she will be okay." She put her notebook and her keys on the dining table and took off her jacket.

"She's my grandmother, not yours," I said.

Anu opened her mouth then changed her mind. "Yes, of course she is yours, Varsha. And I'll bet you're feeling miserable right now. And with flu and all too. Why don't you go up to bed and I'll open the door when your dad gets home."

"No, it's okay," I said. "You don't need to, I can do it."

She shrugged and sat on the sofa. I was dying to sit too. My legs were shivery. But I stood at the window instead, and watched for Papa. He was home in half an hour and started packing to go to the hospital.

"We might have to stay there overnight," he said. "Anu, would you mind sleeping over here with the kids?"

"She doesn't need to, Papa. I'm old enough to be here alone, remember? And if there's something we need help with, I can always go get her from our cottage."

"Don't be absurd, Varsha," Papa snapped, giving me the kind of look he usually keeps for Mama. How could he humiliate me in front of a stranger? He knows what a responsible girl I am. I'm capable, I'm smart, I'm efficient. He's said so a million times. I've taken care of my brother all of his life, haven't I? Watched him being born, changed his diapers, helped Suman with him when she was sick, taken him to school, made sure he eats his lunch and nobody does anything mean to him?

"Not to worry, Vikram," Anu said in her smarmy voice. "You go ahead and look after Akka. We'll be fine here, won't we, Varsha?"

I ignored her.

"Thanks so much, I owe you one," Papa said.

"And I can go get Hemant from the bus stop, not a problem. Now go, we'll be fine. Give us a call after you get there to let us know how she is."

At four o'clock, we left to get Hemant.

"You shouldn't be out in this weather," Anu said, trying to put her hand on my forehead the way Suman does to feel the temperature. Pretending to be my friend.

I brushed her hand off and got into my jacket. "It's not a good idea to be alone out there. There's safety in numbers," I told her. Hem is *my* brother. I didn't want her stealing him from me with sweet talk and T-shirt gifts. *And* he's a blabbermouth. God only knew what he might tell Anu if I wasn't there to stop him.

"That doesn't make any sense, does it?" Anu argued. What does she know? She hasn't lived here all her life, has she? She hasn't seen the kind of winter we have, has she? "I mean, if you're at home, and we don't get back at a reasonable time, at least you can phone for help. Right?"

I shrugged. "I'm going to pick up my brother. You can stay here if you want."

Anu shook her head and followed me out. It was freezing and my breath hung like a ghost in front of my face. The sky was icy white and so low I felt I could reach out and poke my finger through it. We trudged silently towards the bus stop, me on one side of the road and she on the other. I wondered if she could feel how much I hated her.

The bus roared up and stopped. Hem jumped out

bright in his red jacket with the dark blue stripe that Papa bought for him last year, and his new red toque and gloves which are attached to his sleeves with long elastic string so he won't lose them.

"Why is she here?" he demanded. "Where's Mama? What happened to my Mama?"

"Nothing happened to Mama," I said, grabbing his arm. "Come on now, hurry."

"Then where is she?"

"Your grandma fell ill," Anu said, like it was any of her business. "Your parents have taken her to the hospital. I'm going to stay with you until they get home."

"Akka's going to die?" Hem shrilled, his voice high with panic.

"No, she will be fine," Anu said. She held out a hand for him, but I jerked him closer to me.

Hem was quiet for a while, running along beside me. Then he said, "There's a blizzard coming. I can smell it."

"You can?" Anu said. I could almost hear her smiling, making fun of Hem. She doesn't know anything.

"Yes, it's coming from over there." Hem pointed a red finger towards the faraway mountains which were invisible from all the snow that the wind was tossing up.

Our house was waiting for us, the living room window toasty with light. I love seeing the house in winter like that. We rushed inside and Anu offered to make us some hot chocolate.

"There's no need," I told her. "I am perfectly capable of doing it."

She hung up her jacket carefully and turned to me, hands on her waist. "Look, missy, I don't know what your problem is with me, but I have had it up to here!" She stuck her hand up against her eyes. "Now, I'm doing this for Suman's sake and for your Akka—staying here with the two of you. So try to be a bit more pleasant, okay?"

I glared at her. I was going to get back somehow. I hated her then with all my heart.

"Fine," I said. I could pretend too. That she's a friend, not a thief who is planning to take my family away from me. I'm good at pretending.

"Now scoot upstairs and have a lie-down—otherwise we'll have to call the ambulance for you too. Off, off. I'll take care of your brother and fix us some dinner." She smiled at me and I smiled back.

"Hem needs to come upstairs too and change his clothes and have a wash. Then he can have a snack and a glass of chocolate milk. That's how we do it," I told her. "And Mama has already cooked food, so no need for you to make anything."

"Of course, thanks for letting me know. I'll make us all chocolate milk then while you're upstairs." She turned on the lights in the living room and the dining room and the kitchen.

I followed her, turning them all off except for the kitchen and one near the stairs going up.

"What on earth do you think you're doing?" Anu asked.

"Papa said waste not want not. We don't need all those lights."

"Okay, okay, whatever your Papa says. Anything else?"

"And the curtains must remain shut too. That way the heat stays inside the house."

Anu was getting annoyed, I could see. But I didn't care. This is *my* house. I went around the house drawing all the curtains and it was like we were inside a cave.

"Are you mad at me, Varsha?" Hem asked, trailing after me up the stairs to our room. "Why are you mad at me?"

"No, I'm not mad at you."

"Are you mad at Anu? She's making us chocolate milk, that's *nice* of her," said my stupid brother.

"You don't know anything at all, do you, Hem?" I said, dragging him into our room and shutting the door. "She isn't nice, she's a wicked woman."

"But why?" Hem looked at me with his silly round eyes. He had already forgotten the nasty things she had written about us in her notebook.

"She wants to take you and Mama away, that's why."

"Where to?" His eyes got even bigger and he squeaked like a rabbit.

"I don't know."

"Will you come with us?"

"No, Mama can't take me. It would be illegal. And I can't leave Papa alone, can I?"

"But I don't want to leave you," Hem said, holding on to me really tight. "Tell her she can't take us away."

"No, she doesn't know I know," I replied. "And don't go blabbing to her, you hear? I'll figure it out, don't worry."

I wandered over to the window while Hem got out of his school clothes and changed into his pyjamas. It was already dark and the snow was coming down thick and fast, swirling around in the wind, all mixed up with the snow tossed up from the ground. Pretty soon you could see nothing. I was glad we were tight inside our warm house, safe.

We went downstairs and Anu was waiting for us with chocolate milk and a fake smile. Inside, I knew she was plotting and plotting to break up my family.

The phone rang and she picked it up. I ran and grabbed it from her.

"Hi Papa, it's me, Varsha," I said. "How is Akka?"

Another stroke, Papa said. She is deteriorating fast. "We'll be staying here overnight. Be good. I'll see you tomorrow."

Tomorrow. It seemed such a long way off.

"Is Akka dead?" Hem asked tearfully.

"No, no she isn't," I told him. I pulled him into my arms, glad of his baby warmth. "But she might be, pretty soon. She's very old and very sick, you know."

Hem nodded solemnly.

Our tenant stood there looking at us, her face shadowed and creepy, like a mask. She turned on the living room light and became real again.

"Don't," I said to her.

"Don't what?"

"Take away our Mama," I said. "I don't want you to."

She looked stunned. Aha! She thought I didn't hear.

She looked away. Then she turned back to me and said gently, as if I was a moron or something, "I am not *taking* her away, Varsha. If she leaves, she will do it because she wants to. It's her decision. Not mine or, for that matter, yours either."

"I'll tell my father," I threatened.

"And I'll tell the police what he's been doing to all of you," she snapped back.

I didn't know what to say to that. I was so angry. I didn't know what to do. I had to stop her. I had to.

Hemant

I did a sin and I'm scared. I can't sleep. They took Anu away in the dead people's ambulance six days ago. But last night I heard something tapping at my window. Varsha said it's Anu's ghost. *Tap-tappety-tap, open up, let me in, let me in.* She shook up the ice ferns and crystal flowers growing across the glass. I'm scared but Varsha says to ignore her. Like she does. She can see ghosts, all of them, everywhere, crowding into our room, outside near the gate, on the road, at school, in the ice cream shop, they can go everywhere, no passport required. They whisper things but she doesn't look and doesn't hear. That's the trick, she says. To make them go away you need to ignore them. Otherwise they'll grow real and they'll grow strong. So don't look. Another Don't. Must remember. Don't tell, don't look, don't hear.

Varsha came into my room and told me I better keep my mouth shut if I don't want any trouble.

"If you say anything I will tell them the truth. I will tell them what you did," she said.

"But *I* didn't do it!" I was scared of her face close to mine. Her breath was all hot on my face. "*You* did."

"It was you, I saw, you little wuss, it was an accident but it was you. I might have to tell Papa, you know." She kissed my cheek. "Only if you open your mouth. But you won't, will you, Hemu?"

"No, I won't, Varsha, promise, cross my heart and hope to die, hand on your head, in the name of Jesus and Gandhi and Mary and Ganesh, I promise, I won't, I promise."

"If you do, you will go to jail and rot there your whole life. And if you are a wuss and a blabbermouth and if you tell, you will break my heart. And if my heart breaks I will be dead and I won't be able to help you," Varsha said.

"Promise, I won't break your heart, Varsha. I promise."

"You can't tell *anybody*. Promise?"

I can't tell how Anu went out the front door with only her jacket and toque and shoes because she would be back in five minutes.

I can't tell how the cigarette looked just like a red bead in the blizzard night.

I can't tell how we locked the door. I leaned against it so the wind wouldn't push it open and Varsha turned the key.

I can't tell how we switched off the outside light and the lights in the kitchen and on the landing, too, so it was all dark like inside the belly of the whale in Pinocchio.

I can't tell how she banged and cried and howled louder than the wind and still we didn't open the door.

And we didn't open the door. And we didn't and it was so cold.

I can't tell, otherwise I'll be in trouble and go to jail and my sister will die of a broken heart and turn into a ghost and come and eat my brains.

Yesterday night there were lots of ghosts in my room. Varsha said. Grandfather was fuzzy and quiet and he sat on top of my cupboard. He was dressed in a suit and a toque and didn't say anything. He just coughed and coughed and wouldn't stop. And then Varsha saw our baby brother who looked like a tadpole and drowned inside Mama before he was born because she fell on her stomach one night and did something bad to her insides. He crawled out from under the rocking chair. He is harmless and doesn't want to come alive and eat me. Varsha said. Then Anu's ghost came to the window and went *tap-tap-tap*. Varsha said she was asking to be let into the room and should we let her in? I clutched my sister and said *NO. NO. NO.* She was all white and mean-looking. Varsha said. She had snow on her head and her lips were blue.

"She's talking to you," my sister said. "Can you hear her? You can, tell me you can."

I could, I could. Whispering silly, silly, stupid, blabber-mouth, REPULSIVE. I pulled the blanket up over my head and screamed for Mama.

She rushed in. "Oh my poor baby, come here, come here." She hugged me to her and I felt a bit better. But from the corner of my eye I could still see Anu outside the window. She was going to burst through the glass and drown us all in melting snow.

"What's the matter with this stupid boy?" Papa was glaring at me from the door. "Little fool, always blubbering. Are you a boy or a girl?"

"He is only a baby," Mama said. I love the warm feel of her against my face. "Let him be."

"He is a boy," Papa said. "Not a baby."

"What happened, bayboo?" Mama asked, rocking me.

"I saw her," I said. I didn't look at Varsha. I knew she would be mad at me for talking about Anu. I am a blabbermouth and who knows what I will spill by accident.

"Saw who? What's the boy going on about?" Papa said.

"Anu, I saw her." I peeked at Varsha. She was glaring so hard I could feel her eyes digging holes in my head. I know she's going to kill me. She's going to tell Papa that it was me who did it. Then Papa will hit me and I will break my head and it will hurt.

"Oh my poor baby," Mama said. "I shouldn't have let him watch the searchers." She started to cry too and Papa went out of the room. Then Varsha touched Mama on the shoulder and said in her older-child-responsible-person voice, "Mama, don't feel so bad, Mama. Go take a Tylenol and lie down otherwise you will get a headache. I'll take care of Hem."

"No, no, no," I wailed, clinging to Mama. Now I was terrified of my sister. She was mad at me for talking about

Anu. She'd pinch me and summon evil spirits to creep into my ear and torture me.

"It's okay, Hemu, Mama needs to go lie down." Varsha pulled my arms away from Mama and pushed her out of the room. She shut the door and turned to me. "What on earth's wrong with you, Hem? Are you soft in the head or what?"

"But she was here, I promise on Mama's head. I saw her. There, there she is again. She's an iceberg. She's coming to drown us, she'll melt and drown us . . ."

Varsha slapped my face hard so it really hurt. "STOP IT, HEMANT!" she said, her voice sharp but calm like Mrs. Norma's at school. "There is no Anu. She's dead. Remember? Dead dead dead."

"Her ghost, you said we saw her ghost," I cried.

Varsha marched to the window and tapped on it. "Get lost," she said. "Don't bother my brother, you hear me? She's gone now. Look, nothing there."

I stared at the dark window and she was really gone. My sister is stronger than ghosts. It's true. "What if she comes back?"

"She won't, trust me. Do you trust me?"

I nodded.

"Then shut up and stop being a dork, okay?"

"Can I sleep in your room with you tonight?"

"Yes, you can."

"What if she comes to your room?"

"She won't, Hemu." Varsha stroked my damp hair off my forehead.

"How do you know?"

"I know."

"But *how* do you know?"

"Because I'll draw a magic circle around my bed and that will stop all bad spirits from coming near us. Just like the ring that Lakshman drew around Sita to keep the demons away from her."

"Can the other ghosts come into the ring?"

"Nobody can come in." Varsha gave me a shake. "If you don't shut up now I won't let you sleep in my room and I won't draw a magic ring for you."

I stopped crying. My sister is smart and strong. She knows everything. But now I'm afraid of the ghosts *and* her.

"But remember, you must always listen to me and do what I say. Otherwise I can't be responsible for what happens to you. So are you going to tell?"

"What if it comes out by itself?"

"It won't. Okay, you can tell Tree if you want. I don't mind that. You can say it was a mistake. You can say you're sorry."

I nodded, but I don't want to tell Tree. I want to tell Mama. She's *my* Mama, not Varsha's, and she'll believe me. She'll take care of me. I'll CONFESS. Nicky Hutch's mother who is a Catholic person goes to church and confesses her sins and god forgives her. I'll confess otherwise I'll go to hell and hang upside down and get boils on my penis and my eardrums will burst and blood will come out from everywhere and I will be in great pain forever.

Mama won't tell Varsha, but Varsha will find out—she always finds out. If I don't tell Mama, I'll burst into pieces like the fat lady full of secrets whose story Akka told us a long time ago when I was little.

Suman

Then came the sad business of informing Anu's family. There is a brother in Vancouver and an elderly mother. What an awful responsibility, what a miserable task. I pulled open the dresser drawer in the kitchen to look for phone numbers. Should I call, or should I leave it to Vikram?

An envelope surfaced from the mess of string and keys and pieces of paper stuffed into the drawer. It had Anu's writing on it. I remembered her bringing it over a couple of weeks ago, when she arrived for her usual afternoon tea and a chat, to show Akka and me some photographs. She had forgotten to take them back, and I had tucked the envelope into the drawer meaning to return them to her the following morning. Then Akka fell ill and the envelope slipped from my mind.

I opened it expecting to find Anu's photographs, but instead there was a single picture of us—Akka, Vikram, Hem, Varsha and me—and on the back, in a childish scrawl, the legend *Our Family*. It was Hem's writing, but surely not his idea to take away Anu's photographs? Must have been Varsha, but I can never tell, they seem to be one brain in two bodies.

"What did you do with Anu's photographs?" I asked, catching them on their way out into the yard.

"We threw them away, Mama," Varsha said. Her face was flushed and innocent, her dark hair had strayed out of her bright pink toque which I knitted for her and which she always wears to show me how much she likes it.

"Why? Why did you do that? They were hers, you had no business." I was so upset. I tried to keep the anger out of my voice.

"But she is dead, Mama," Varsha replied. "She won't care anyway."

"And she wasn't part of our family," Hem added, and received one of those quick nudges from Varsha, after which he didn't open his mouth again.

"Yes, she wasn't family, but she has a brother and a mother and other people who might have wanted the pictures—they are her most recent photographs. How would *you* feel if somebody took your things?" I wanted to slap them both.

"I would hate them for*ever*," Varsha said, glowering at me. Then, in that way she has that can change the mood in the room suddenly, she smiled. "We can get the photographs back if you want, Mama. We haven't thrown them away yet, not properly, that is. Right, Hem?"

He shook his head.

"Yes, I would like that. I have to pack her things for her family," I said.

Varsha beamed at me again. "Is there anything to eat, Mama? I am starving!"

"Yeah, starving!" Hem echoed, grinning too. But he is still uneasy. I can smell his fear.

Later still, looking out of the kitchen window, I saw them both at the far end of the backyard, their faces pressed against the tree, spilling out their hearts to it. I wonder what they were whispering to it.

They turned suddenly as if they could feel my gaze on them, stood there poised like the deer that wander out of the woods. Hemant waved to me. Then Varsha caught his arm and pulled him behind her, around the house, and they disappeared from sight. I know Hem is concealing something. I have to catch him alone, and quickly, before Varsha works on him, convinces him not to tell me. The influence that girl has on my son is not healthy. I am beginning to feel Anu was right—I have to take him away from here.

The rest of the morning passed in a haze. Vikram took the responsibility of phoning Anu's brother, for which I was grateful. It was left to me to pack her belongings for her brother to take back with him. I dragged her empty suitcases out of the cupboard in Akka's room where I'd stored them and headed out to the back-house. It looked small and lost in the snowy landscape. I thought, not for the first time, that there is too much unused land surrounding the house. It could accommodate, quite luxuriously, the entire street where I spent my childhood. I imagine it crowded with my old neighbours, their children and grandchildren, beggars and fruit vendors, cobblers and thieves, the oil merchants and cloth-shop owners, the candle-makers, bangle sellers, laundry women, idlers, rogues—they would create a warm, merry little scene here until this winter chill crept into their unwary bones. Oh yes, in this place winter is always lurking around the corner, a wicked creature roaming these lonely spaces, waiting to pounce on your bones, freeze your blood. But Anu did not understand winter the way we do—she had never really lived inside it, she did not know how cunning the cold can be. How I wish now that I had warned her more forcefully!

I unlocked the door with the keys Anu had left on our dining table—I couldn't understand why she bothered to lock it—and waited for a few moments. I was ready to believe she was still around, that she hadn't left in that ambulance. Everything was exactly the way it was the last time I had stopped by with my offering of hot lunch: the sofa bed piled high with pillows and comforters, the round table with her books neatly piled, the wooden armoire in the corner, and the kitchenette with a tea kettle poised on the stove, waiting.

I wandered around the small space collecting the things she had left behind:

—A pile of empty notebooks. I searched but could not find the one in which she was always scribbling her stories. Her family would like to have that, I felt sure.

I wonder whether it too is somewhere out there, buried in the snow, whether it will surface in spring, a soggy tattered thing full of Anu's thoughts.

—1,350 dollars in a pouch, eight dollars in coins in a jar. I hesitated and slipped it all into the pocket of my jacket. I feel ashamed and guilty about it. But then I believe she would have lent it to me anyway, she had offered her help so generously, so what is the harm in taking it now she's gone? When I'm settled into a different life, I will send it back to her brother's address.

—Some junk jewellery and a single heavy gold bangle which her mother gave her when she got married. Unlike the money, it had sentimental value, and I had no doubt it should return to her family.

—A wedding ring that she kept after she got divorced.

—Car keys, pens, books she loved, random items that litter our lives. I threw them all into the suitcase.

—Clothes: white blouse, red blouse, three skirts (one with pink flowers she liked a lot), four jeans, four trousers, underwear. Three pairs of shoes.

—Photographs of her brother and his children and of her parents when they were young, a long time ago.

The old refrigerator started up suddenly with a groan and my heart jumped in alarm. I cleaned its contents out into a garbage bag, took one last look around the room and tramped back through the snow to my house.

I feel enormously sad. I have lost a friend. It will be two friends when Akka dies—which won't be long now. It is time to make a decision. A long time ago, on the roof

of an old house in Agra, I contemplated that thin little
word—*I*. Can I fulfill its potential, I wonder, can I push
it as tall and as wide as it can go, that slender word? It's
time now to find my lost self, that scrawny *I* that fell
into a mirror that moonlit night. It's time to drag myself
out of this mirror in which I've trapped myself, time to
let myself go.

It is now a week after Anu's death. Her things have all
gone, carried away by her brother, and the back-house is
empty once more. I'm alone except for Hem, who has
stayed home from school, complaining of a stomach ache.
I don't question him—her death has upset him deeply,
I know. He wakes up screaming at night, insisting there
are ghosts knocking at the windows. He's outside playing
now, and through the kitchen window I can see him,
bright against the snow in his red winter jacket, his arms
wrapped around the large tree a little to the left of the
back-house. He looks a bit like he's hanging on for dear
life. I tap on the window to summon him back inside—
he is sick, he shouldn't be outside for too long. He turns
around at the sound and stumbles frantically through the
snow towards the house. I open the door to let him in
and he falls into my arms.

"I heard her," he sobs. "I *heard* her."

I am bewildered. "Who did you hear, bayboo?"

"Anu. I *heard* her just now. Tap-tap, she was tapping
on the window."

I shake my head and pull him into the warmth of the

kitchen. Hug him tight and rock him like I used to when he was a baby. "That was me, not Anu. It was me."

He holds tight to me and sobs even louder. "Mama," he says. "Mama, I have a secret, a bad secret."

SECRETS

I have a secret. I tell Mama . . .

I tell Mama how when she and Papa went to stay with Akka in the hospital, and Anu came over to look after me and Varsha, we turned off all the lights in the house except three. And when Anu asked what we were doing we told her Papa doesn't like to waste electricity. Then Varsha pulled all the curtains shut and Anu asked what we were doing and we said that way the heat stays inside the house.

Then we told Anu we were going upstairs so I could do my homework and Varsha could take a nap because she was sick. And Varsha said I must not to speak one single word to Anu. "Did you hear? She said Mama was going to leave us. Did you hear? She is going to take our Mama away from us. She is *not* a good person."

"Is Mama going to leave me too?" I asked.

Varsha hit me on my back so hard I nearly fell on my face. "What's so special about you, stupid? She is going to leave *all* of us and go away."

Then we went downstairs again and had dinner and after everything was all cleaned up and Anu did the dishes she asked if we wanted to play Monopoly or something. We didn't speak one single word. Varsha said not to. Anu was going to steal our mother. So Anu shook her head, stuck her hands on her waist and said, "Okay you two, what's with the silent treatment?"

We didn't say anything.

Anu shook her head again. "Have it your way. I'm going out for a smoke."

She opened the door and the blizzard pushed the wind in. It was cold cold cold and snow was pouring down from the sky and it was dark black outside. Anu said *brrr* and stepped back in to zip up her jacket and pull on her toque.

"Will I need my gloves do you think?" she asked.

It was freezing cold, there was a storm, *of course* she needed gloves and scarf and snow pants.

"It's kind of hard to hold a cigarette with paws though, eh?" It was like she was talking to herself since we weren't saying anything. "So maybe not." She turned to us. "Okay you two darlings, don't do anything naughty in the next five minutes, hear me? Yes? No? Oh fine, have it your way." She went out and pulled the door shut behind her. It became warm again.

"Stupid cow," Varsha said. She turned the key in the door. Then ran into the kitchen and turned off the light and pulled down the blinds. Came back to the landing and switched off the light there too, and the outside light which our Papa had said to always always keep on.

"What are you doing?" I asked. I couldn't see any-thing, not even my hand, it was so dark. Darker than inside my closed eyes. "Why are you switching off all the lights? I'm scared."

"Nonsense," Varsha said. "Why are *you* scared? *You* aren't outside there are you? Now shut up and sit here with me."

We sat in the dark and then the knocking started up. *Tap-tap, tap-tap,* Anu went. And then when we didn't open the door she went *Bang Bang Bang.* And still we didn't open and I was crying and saying it's so cold we should open the door Varsha, we should open the door. She will be eaten up by the snow, I cried. I wanted Varsha to switch on the lights and open the door so Anu could come back in. But my sister said, "Shh, shh, it's okay Hem, she needs to learn a lesson, that's all."

Then she took my hand and slowly, bumping into stuff, we went to Akka's room and crept under her smelly blanket and waited for tomorrow.

"If anyone asks, Hem," Varsha whispered, cuddling close to me, "if anyone asks, just say we were fast asleep."

I tell Mama we shut the door and turned off the lights and left Anu outside in the blizzard when it was freezing cold. I tell her how we didn't open the door. I tell her how we found Anu's notebook where she left it on the table with her keys. I said we shouldn't take it but Varsha said finders-keepers so now it was ours. She hid it in a secret place inside her cupboard so Papa can't find out about Anu helping Mama run away, and about how she's going to take only me and not Varsha. If he found out he would be broken-hearted. Varsha said. And if his heart broke he might go mad and do something bad to us. Varsha said.

I tell her how Anu's ghost bangs every night and day on my room window and on the windows of all the rooms and I can't sleep because I'm scared she's coming to get me. I'm scared of my sister and Papa, and I cry that I want to go far away from here with her. And I tell her where Varsha hid her passport. I tell her *every*thing.

And then I feel bad that I BETRAYED Varsha.

So I go tell Tree what I just did. And Tree tells Varsha.

And now my sister knows I told on her. She knows *every*thing.

I have a secret. I am leaving . . .

Hemu has told me. I find it hard to believe that two children could do what they did. No—*one* child. My son isn't responsible. He is a baby. Too young to resist that girl. That terrible, terrible girl.

He also told me my passport is hidden behind the photograph of Mr. J.K. Dharma. Varsha stuck it there because she was afraid I would leave her. I think of that day years ago when she told me that she would rather have me dead, a garlanded photograph on the wall with the rest of her family, than let me go. I thought it was childish rage. Now I know it was not. She is mad. I feel sorry for her, but now I know I cannot stay here and allow my son to be turned into someone like her. Anu was right, I have to get out, I owe it to my child. And to myself. It will be difficult, but I will manage. I have made up my mind and that is a start.

I stare out of the kitchen window at the back-house, so dark and lonely. Out of the corner of my eye I spot a flutter of pink. It is Varsha, back from school. Hem follows, holding her hand, dragging behind. For the first time, she insisted she could come back on her own today. "It's okay, Mama," she said, kissing me sweetly this morning. "I can bring Hem home by myself. I am old enough."

Vikram wasn't there to object to this—he's in the hospital with Akka. She is failing fast, any day now, she will be gone, the doctors have said. All the more reason for me to leave this house, this family.

Hem breaks away from Varsha and stumbles through the snow towards me. Varsha grabs his jacket, hauls him back and leans into him. He squirms out of her grasp and continues towards me. Varsha stands there alone, her toque bright against the winter whiteness, and then she heads to that giant tree they both love so much. She leans against it, her face close to the trunk. I used to wish I could ask the tree what the children were whispering to it, what they were burying in its ancient wooden heart, and now I am not sure I ever want to know.

Varsha finishes her conversation with the tree and turns towards the house, looks up and catches sight of me at the kitchen window. She stands still and looks straight at me. I wave to her. She does not respond. I wave again. It is better to pretend I don't know. Soon she will be inside the house with us, this girl who is capable of anything. Inside the house her grandfather built on a road that goes nowhere, in a place where nobody cares what happens behind the closed doors of a house. Where family business is the business of the family.

I have a secret . . .

I shut the door. And turned the key. And switched off the lights.

I know the passport isn't where I hid it. Suman found it. Hem told me—he can't keep a secret, the silly blabbermouth. I know Suman is going to leave. Hem told me that too. I know she will take my brother with her. But he is *mine. I* saw him first. Akka is gone. There is nobody else left for me. Suman cannot go. She can't take my brother. I will have to find a way to keep her here forever. To keep Hem with me. I *will* find a way.

I am cunning as the snow.

I am sharp as the winter wind.

I am strong as Tree.

I can find a way.

I am Varsha Dharma, granddaughter of Mr. J.K. Dharma (late), and Bhagirathi Bai (late), daughter of Vikram and Harini alias Helen (late), stepdaughter of Suman, sister of Hem. This is *my* house, this is *my* family.

Acknowledgements

This is a wholly inadequate acknowledgement of my debt to the following people:

— Louise Dennys for her insightful editorial guidance, patience, and wonderful ability to draw the best possible out of me

— Deirdre Molina for her equally perceptive comments and sharp eye for detail

— Denise Bukowski for her strong support through endless drafts and her faith in me

— all my wonderful friends at Knopf Canada who have had a hand in sending this book out into the world.

ANITA RAU BADAMI's first novel was the bestseller *Tamarind Mem*. Her bestselling second novel, *The Hero's Walk*, won the Regional Commonwealth Writers' Prize and Italy's Premio Berto, was named a Washington Post Best Book, was long-listed for the International IMPAC Dublin Literary Award and the Orange Prize for Fiction, and was a finalist for the Kiriyama Prize. Her third novel, *Can You Hear the Nightbird Call?*, was released in 2006 to great acclaim, longlisted for the IMPAC Award, and a finalist for the City of Vancouver Book Award. The recipient of the Marian Engel Award for a woman writer in mid-career, Badami is also a visual artist. She lives in Montreal.

The body of *Tell It to the Trees* has been set in Monotype Garamond, a modern font family based on roman types cut by Jean Jannon in 1615. Jannon followed the designs of Claude Garamond, cut a century earlier. Garamond's types were in turn based on the work of Francesco Griffo in the late 15th century. Monotype Garamond's italics are derived from types designed in France circa 1557 by Robert Granjon.